In the Irish past

ETHNA CARBERY

GW00492628

THE MERCIER PRESS
DUBLIN and CORK

The
The Mercier Press Limited
4 Bridge Street, Cork
25 Lower Abbey Street, Dublin 1

ISBN O 85342 546 9

CONTENTS

THE SORROWING OF CONAL CEARNACH

The autumn night had set in with a dreary darkness full of the howling of angry winds that swept up from the sea, and flung clouds of salt foam even to the crest of the gray cliffs that stood sentinel over the Northern coast of Uladh. White screaming flocks of seagulls darted inland, flying low, as is their wont when the storm-fiend comes to take his pleasure; and in scanty hedge or stunted fir-tree the little timid land-birds cowered before the blast. The air held the chill of coming winter; the moaning waters seemed to chant a dirge for all the dead whose bones lay far beneath among the weeds and wrecks and tossing shells; and overhead the thick clouds went drifting by without the glimmer of a single star to light the gloom, while, through this maze of storm and darkness, with sorrow in his heart and on his brow, after his many and perilous wanderings over distant countries, Conal Cearnach, the chieftain of Dunseverick, and Champion of the Red Branch Knights of Uladh, came back to his own.

But though the storm might sport and rave in ecstacy as it circled the open coast-line, it seemed to shriek its madness round the towers of the Caiseal, which stood but a short way from the brink of a tall cliff that sheered straight down into the foaming wild water. It hissed and swirled through the broad open chimney of the banqueting hall, scattering the flames in the heart of the glowing logs piled high upon the hearth, and sending showers of light peat ashes almost to the feet of Conal Cearnach himself, who, sitting silent in his carven chair of dark oak, with mournful eyes gazing steadily at the leaping fire, heeded neither the rattle, as each fresh gust hurled itself against the timbers of the walls, nor the chanting of his harper, nor yet the sweet voice of his lady as she strove to win him from the bitter thoughts that held him in that sad and woeful quietude. Many and melodious were the strains by which the harper sought to rouse his master; now soft and silvery as the thrush's warble in the glow of a mellow summer eve; anon bursting into loud and triumphant pealing like the return of a victor army from the field of conflict, and again sinking into melting harmony as when a mother croons at slumber-hour above the baby on her bosom. Clear and tuneful the song rose with the harp-music, telling of Conal Cearnach's wonderful and world-enduring feats; of his manly beauty and his valour; of his loyalty to friend and vengefulness to foe, of the glorious attributes that had raised him to the Champion's place in the Court of the Red Branch, and won him renown at home and afar as the flower of Uladh's matchless chivalry. Loudly and proudly did the music-maker chant the death of Misgedhra, the great soldier, slain single-handed in a trial of skill by the Chieftain of Dun-severick. Solemnly he related the making of the brain-ball of that valiant fighter, and how the dead had been revenged upon Uladh afterwards, when this ghastly trophy, that belonged to Conal Cearnach by right of prowess, and was lodged for safety in the royal palace of Crovdearg, passed into the hands of the enemy through the hands of a fool, and brought about the gravest sorrow under which Uladh had ever bowed, in the death of her gifted and noble ruler Conor Mac Nessa. And as he sang the death-lament for Conor, the warriors ranged all down the long hall took up the strain, and mingled their praise and regret for the kingly king with the twanging of the harp until the sob of the wind seemed hushed outside and the hissing of the waters died away. Then in the distant chamber of the Lady of Dunseverick her waiting women and maidens, hearing this weird and mounful chanting, took up the *caoine*, and shrill-ed the dead man's praises with clapping of palms and rending of hair, until, in sooth, throughout the Caiseal from end to end no sounds but those of grief and dismay echoed

6

on this the return-night of the Chieftain. Once, and once only, was his brooding gaze lifted, and his brows arched, not in anger, but in surprise, as he asked curiously—

'Wherefore this clamour in my halls tonight? There seems but storm without and storm within, and it vexeth me. Hush ye, hush ye, my people.'

The harper rose, flushing red because of the reproof, and vouchsafed a reply.

'It was the death-lament for Conor the King we sang, my honoured lord, and inasmuch as he hath died but a short time since, we feared you sorrowed for him in silence. And because our battle-stains or strains of love have been powerless to win you from your grief, in our affection we have fallen in with this mood, and have joined in your regrets. The death he died was a strange one, and unknown in all the annals of the land.'

'I, too, have looked on death,' said Conal Cearnach, slowly and reverently, still gazing into the burning brightness on the hearth, 'but not such a death as a King of Eirinn might die. Nay, 'twas such as only a God could endure and make no moan. A great end and a terrible. Yet the divine pity in His eyes bore naught but forgiveness for those who tortured Him, and their dying glory hath made me His slave for ever.'

'My lord, my lord,' pleaded his wife, rising and clasping her white arms round his neck, 'put these haunting thoughts away, I pray thee, and turn to the feast where thy kin and clan await to give thee welcome home. Tell us how thou didst bear thyself at Rome, and of thy wrestling feats in those far distant cities. Thou wert champion swordsman there as well as here, my love and brave knight, were thou not? They indeed had courage who accepted the challenge of Conal Cearnach and strove to match their strength with his. Sad for Ceat was the day when he met thee; he that was ever a champion of renown. Sing, harper, sing the death of Ceat,- son of Magach of Connacht, that my lord may remember only his own great fame and forget this grief that holds him enchained.'

Once more the harper ran his fingers across the strings, breaking into high, proud chanting. The oft-told tale, ever new because of their joy in it, brought a glint of battle-fury into the eyes of all those listening warriors. Only the Chieftain heeded not, though well he might have gloried in that marvellous recital. How Ceat came out of Connacht to fight the stoutest champions of Uladh, and how he slew three of them, one by one, in single combat. And setting forth with their heads as trophies to show to his own people he was pursued by the Chieftain of Dunseverick and overtaken at Athceitt. Then the bloodiest and most furious combat that had ever been known in Eirinn took place between these two. Shields were pierced and swords were hacked, and many men died that day, but it was left to the two champions to decide the issue of war. And the victory was with Uladh, for after many most wonderful exploits Ceat of Connacht fell by the hand of Conal Cearnach, who, pierced with wounds, lay well-nigh dead himself upon the field. The song told how Conal was carried into Connacht by Bealchue Breifne and tended until his strength was restored to him, when, for fear of his strong arm and following, his host sought to put the Ultonian to death, repenting that he had saved him. How Conal baffled the treacherous schemers, and made his way back to Uladh, all was chanted, and chorused and cheered. But still the hero sat silent, taking no pride, as of yore, in his own exploits, and slowly the voices sank, the harping ended in a few faint silvery echoes, and all grew mournful because of the brooding eyes of their lord.

*　　*　　*　　*　　*

This was the vision that Conal Cearnach saw in the heart of the fire that night of his return to Dunseverick.

He saw himself at the beginning of this, the most curious adventure that had yet befallen him, setting forth with a strong, well-chosen band, on a foray into Britain, a country lying beyond a narrow sea to the east of the land of Eirinn.

Many were the tales that had reached his ears and the ears of other warriors of Uladh concerning the descent of the mighty, world-famed Romans upon this island; how they had exhibited to the people their much-vaunted feats of athletic skill until the report of their daring and courage had penetrated the Court of Emania.

What wonder that the war-like hot blood of Conal Cearnach pulsed to hear the deeds of the Roman soldiers, that he longed to try his strength with theirs on battle field or in the field of sport. And when he had come amongst them, and they noted his great height, his agile limbs, and the muscles that swelled adown the length of his powerful arms, their admiration and awe of him surpassed all bounds. Easily did he overthrow the stalwart wrestlers sent from the Roman ranks against him; easily did he bear away the victor's palm at the hurling of weights and enormous stones; and more easily still did he excel their highest leaps by the swift-darting of his strong and beautiful body. Then, ere their exclamations had time to die away, he rose once more into the air in his last and most marvellous feat—the salmon-sault; shooting up like that great fish from a river, turning over in his flight once and twice, and coming down to earth again as surely and as swiftly as the salmon might dive into the broad river from which it had sprung so boldly.

But envy as well as admiration grew in the hearts of the Romans, and they said, 'Wert thou in our arena at Rome thou had'st met thy master, all powerful as thou art, O Conal. Come with us for thy fame's sake, that thou may'st have tales to tell thy children when the gray is on thy hair—if our gladiators let thee live so long.' And the Lord of Dunseverick took up the challenge, sailing from Britain in the company of these world-compelling foreigners, far from his northern home and loving clansmen.

Then the vision changed, and he seemed to see again the wide arena and the crowds of eager faces that watched the mighty wrestlers as they strained and struggled, tight locked in each other's embrace. He felt the long arms of the huge gladiator go round him like a ring of steel—a grand and gigantic figure of equal height with himself, to whom victory would have come readily had his opponent been other than the flower of the Red Branch Chivalry. Across the arena they wrestled, now on foot, now bent on knee, sending showers of sand high into the air, while cries of praise or blame broke from thousands of throats, aye, and from Imperial Caesar too, as the Roman strove to end the contest. But the battle-fury had fallen upon Conal, as it fell on him that time he slew the King of Leinster at Atha-Cliath, and he put forth suddenly his own renowned strength for the final wrestle. He noted how a tremor of strained agony then ran through the frame of the other; how his blood-shot eye-balls rolled, and the beads of sweat gathered on brow and cheek until his bones creaked under the stress of the champion's hold, and his lifeless head fell backwards over his crushed and blackened shoulder. And Conal wore that day upon his ruddy head the palm-crown of the victor.

Again the vision shifted and changed, and he saw himself the comrade of a band of centurions, who had journeyed over land and sea in peaceful wise to the populous and glowing cities of the East. It was afternoon of a certain day when they reached Jerusalem, the city of the Jews, a strange day and a fearful, for the sun hung like a ball of fire in the heavens, and the air was filled with the noise of shouting men and the wailing of women. Past the bare and brown synagogues the strangers went, following the track of hurrying crowds that stayed not for question or reply, so intent were they on the purpose that drew them onward. Here and there a group of women talked in whispers, pausing at sight of the Romans and the splendidly-clad chieftain of Uladh, whose like they had never gazed upon before. For Conal Cearnach wore his wide-spreading scarlet cloak, fastened with a large brooch of gold, across his breast, and his ruddy hair fell down in many plaits to his broad shoulders, each plait being tied at the end by a string and tiny ball of gold. His short trimmed beard was ruddy as his hair, his cheeks were like an apple when the sun hath kissed

10

it, and his blue bright eyes, keen-glacing, drew the eyes of all to look at him.

And the Jewish women hushed their talk as he came up the way to marvel at his height and grandeur, and it was then that the centurions, seeking speech of them, learned what had so disturbed the wonted customs of the city.

'It is One whom they go to crucify on Golgotha,' said the women. 'A Man who hath called Himself the Son of God, and we know not if the deed they do be just or wise.'

'What crime hath He done?'

'Nay, no crime, unless crime it be to raise the dead to life, or restore sight to the blind, or hearing to the deaf, or give strength to the lame and feeble, and comfort to the sad of heart. All this He hath done, for we have seen it; and there are many who have followed Him in the belief that He is the long-looked-for Messiah, whom the prophets have foretold.'

'And is it for this the Jews have given Him to death?'

'Yea,' answered the women, 'and because that He hath spoken of the Kingdom of His Father and of Himself as King of the Jews.'

'Then He deserves death for *that* saying,' cried the Centurions, 'for Caesar, and Caesar alone, is your king. We go to see Him die. What name hath He?'

'Jesus of Nazareth.'

Up the steep stony road that led to Calvary Conal Cearnach went with his Roman companions. Here and there he noted drops of blood upon the pathway, as they hastened onward with such speed that the crowds gave way before them, and the little black-eyed Jewish children drew aside from their course in terror. Once they stopped before a weeping woman, shrouded in a long dark cloak, across whose knees as she sat was stretched a blood-stained towel, upon which her tears fell thick as rain, and over which many people were bending. Then they saw that the towel bore the impress in lines of blood of a most sad and weary Face—'the Face of Him Who is being crucified,' said a by-stander, in answer to their looks of wonder. 'This woman

11

wiped the sweat from His Brow as He passed by, and His Face is here as a memento of Him whom Pilate hath called "that just Man".'

Into the soul of Conal the hot anger came rushing as he broke away from the centurions and sped like a blast of wind towards the mount where the people had assembled. One thought filled his mind, 'Shall I be nigh and witness the torture of this Man, whose only crime hath been the good that He hath done? Nay, it were not known in Emania that many should fall upon one; it is the trial of single combat we give even to our enemies. I shall be His champion to the death if He will take me for such.'

Yet, alas, and alas! it was a bleeding and dying Christ that hung upon the cross when the Chieftain of Dunseverick drew near and stood beneath. And as he gazed in horror at the dastard deed, a soldier coming up in haste pierced the Victim's side with a spear so that the Blood shot forth and trickled down the rough wood upon which they had nailed Him. And a drop touched the brow of Conal Cearnach ere he knew, and the fury left him for a marvellous and unwonted peace while he watched the Saviour die. Then rocks were rent and graves opened, so that the dead came forth in their cerements in that most awful hour; and lightnings flashed from the black thick clouds that had suddenly covered the sky, and all was dread and unearthly, so that the people shrieked and crouched upon the ground repentant and sore afraid.

'It was indeed a God who died,' said the chieftain sadly and slowly, 'this cruel and untimely death. My grief, oh! my bitter grief, that the Red Branch Knights were afar, else a sure and fierce revenge would overtake these Jews, aye, their city should be levelled and their name effaced had the chivalry of Uladh been here this day with sword and skian and blue-black lance to hold the battle straight with me.'

*　　*　　*　　*　　*

This was the memory that Conal Cearnach dwelt upon the night he returned through storm and darkness, after many wanderings, to his Caiseal of Dunseverick on the bleak sea-swept Northen coast of Uladh.

NOTE.—The tradition that Conal Cearnach of Dunseverick was present at Jerusalem on the day of the Crucifixion is still preserved amongst the peasantry of the Glens of Antrim. I have never been able to find a written record of this, save in a note to the 'Wars of the Gaedhil and the Gall', which merely mentions the legend. It is also said that Conal was at the burial of Christ as well, and that he put his shoulder to raise the lid of the sepulchre when Joseph of Arimathea made it ready for the reception of the Body of our Lord. Taking it for granted that this Champion of the Red Branch Knights did actually exist so long ago, we can well believe in his journey to Rome with the Romans who had landed in Britain, and his subsequent feats in the Arena, and his further travels throughout the Holy Land. It was decreed that a representative of every race on the earth should be present at the Death upon Mount Calvary, and the tradition that has been lovingly entwined around the heroic name of the Chieftain of Dunseverick ought to be known and treasured by the Irish people. Dunseverick lies on the northern coast of County Antrim, not far from Portrush.

THE TRAVELLING SCHOLARS

Upon the wind-swept bosom of Loch Lein, in the Kingdom of Kerry, lie many beautiful and well-wooded islands, where birds sing at dawn and twilight most enchanting strains. Very sweet and far-reaching is their singing, silvery and heart-moving, tender and jubilant, a paean of grateful praise to the Lord of the sky and earth and sea. And Echo, the Son of the Rock, steals out of his fastnesses to listen, and enraptured joins his voice to the concert of rippling melody until the tremulous warble of the birds is hurled strong and loud across the blue waters, down misty glen and deep ravine; over slow rivers winding through green meadow-lands, to die away at last above the cloud-capped crest of the distant purple mountains.

But the loveliest of all these lovely islands, where song-birds have their home among blossoms and fluttering leaves, is Innisfallen, the fairy isle. Here is was that Saint Finan built his great monastery in the ages long ago, and here did Maelsoohan O'Carroll rule as eminent scholar and chief Doctor of the western world during the reign of Brian the Ard-righ of Erin. It was by Maelsoohan that Brian in his boyhood was educated and taught the duties of a king, and in after years when the renowned Dalcassian was monarch over all the land, mindful of the love and reverence his heart held ever towards the teacher of his youth, he sent for the sage, and raised him to to the dignity of Anmchara or Counsellor to the King. It was during this period that the event which I am about to relate occcurred; a wonderful tale and a true one.

There came one day, at the same hour, three students from Connor, in Ulster, to receive education from Maelsoohan O'Carroll in his monastery on Innisfallen. These three students resembled each other in figure, in features, and in their name, which was Domnall. They remained three years learning with him, and their talent was so marvellous that his pride in them became very great. At the end of the three years they said to their preceptor—'It is our desire to go to Jerusalem, in the land of Judea, that our feet may tread every path our Saviour walked in when on earth. This is our wish, oh master, and we pray thee hinder us not, but give us thy blessing, and let us go.' And while his heart was sad at parting with them Maelsoohan made answer—'You shall not go until you have left with me the reward of my labour.'

In grief and amazement the pupils said, 'We have not anything that we can give you, oh master, to compensate for all the care and affection you have spent upon us, but we will remain three years more to serve you humbly if it be your will.' 'I do not wish that,' replied the sage, 'but I have a demand to make, which you shall grant, or my curse will rest heavy upon you.'

'Name it,' said they, 'and if it lies within our power we shall do what you decree.'

Then Maelsoohan bound them by an oath on the Gospel of the Lord that their promise might be kept. 'You shall go and make your pilgrimage in the path that your souls desire,' said he, 'and you shall die, at the same time, all together. The demand I require from you is that you wend not to heaven after your deaths, until you have first visited me, to tell me the length of my life and whether I shall obtain the peace of the Lord.'

'We promise you all this,' said the three, 'for the sake of the Lord,' and leaving him their blessing they departed.

In due time they reached the land of Judea, and walked in the footsteps of the Saviour. They came at last to Jerusalem, and there death overtook them, all three together at the same hour, as their master had foretold, and they were buried with much honour in that holy place. Then Michael the Archangel came from God for them, but they said—'We will not go until we have fulfilled the promise which we made to our preceptor, under our oaths on the Gospel of Christ.'

'Go,' commanded the angel, 'and tell him that he has three years and a half to live, and that he goes to hell for all eternity after the sentence of the Day of Judgment.'

'And wherefore?'

'For three causes,' replied the angel—'namely, because of how much he interpolates the canon, and because of his love for women, and also for having abandoned the Altus.'*

The reason why Maelsoohan abandoned the Altus was this. He had a very good son named Maelpatrick, who became seized with a mortal sickness, and the Altus was seven times sung round him that he should not die. This was, however, of no avail, since the son died forthwith, and the father then declared that he would no longer sing the hymn, as he did not see that God honoured it. Therefore Maelsoohan had been seven years without singing the Altus when his three pupils came to talk to him in the form of white doves.

'Tell me,' said he, 'what shall be the length of my life, and if I shall receive the heavenly reward?'

'You have,' replied they, 'three more years to live, and after that time you go to hell for ever.'

'Why should I go to hell?' queried Maelsoohan, in great awe and wonderment.

'For three causes,' and they related to him the three causes already known.

'It is not true that I shall go to the place of the wicked.' said their master, 'for those three vices that are mine this day shall not be mine even this day, nor shall they be mine from this time forth, for I will abandon these vices, and God will forgive me for them, as He Himself has promised,

* The Altus.—This was the celebrated poem or hymn written by Saint Columcille at Iona in honour of the Trinity, when the messengers of Pope Gregory came to him with the great cross and other presents.

when he said—"The impiety of the impious, in whatever hour he shall be turned from it, shall not injure him." I will put no sense of my own into the canons, but such as I shall find in the Divine Books. I will perform a hundred genuflections every day. Seven years have I been without singing the Altus; now I will sing it seven times every night while I live; and I will keep a three days' fast every week. Go you now to heaven, and come back on the day of my death to tell me the result.'

'We will come,' they promised, so the three departed as they came, first leaving a blessing with him, and receiving his blessing in return.

When, at the end of three years, Maelsoohan lay on his death-bed, the three pupils appeared to him in the same forms—that of white doves. They saluted him, and he returned their salutations, saying—'Is my life the same before God as it was on the former day when you came to talk to me, oh my children?' and they replied—

'It is not, indeed, the same, for we were shown your place in heaven, and we are satisfied with its goodness. We are now here, as we promised, to take you with us to the place which is prepared for you that you may be in the presence of God, in the unity of the Trinity, and of the hosts of heaven, till the Day of Judgment.'

There were assembled about Maelsoohan many priests and ecclesiastics; he was anointed, and his pupils parted not with him until they all went to heaven together. And in the Monastery of Innisfallen, on Loch Lein, there was exceeding sorrow and regret because of the loss of so learned and holy a man. But in the truly wonderful books he had compiled the priest and scholars found much food for study and reflection in after years; hence it is that the name and fame of Maelsoohan O'Carroll is handed down even to us of this day as a sage Doctor of far-extending renown—the preceptor and counsellor of Brian Boroimbhe, Ard-righ of Erin, and victor of the bloody field of Cluaintairbh.

PURSUIT OF DIARMUID AND GRAINNE

It was told to me by a warrior of the Fiana Eirinn, he who afterwards became thy father, O little prattling ones, how Fionn in the mighty passion of his anger, when the magic sleep had passed away from the wedding-guests in the banqueting hall of King Cormac Mac Art, gathered his great host around him, and gave chase to my Princess Grainne and Diarmuid O'Duibhne. Of a surety it would have proved an ill flight for the lovers had they been friendless in this hour of their need, but the hearts of Fionn's army, save a few, were with them, and Angus Oge the Immortal, the foster-father of Diarmuid, followed unseen in the wake from the palace of Tara.

Fast and furious did Fionn ride upon their track until he came to the Ford of Athlone, over against the Shannon river. Here the flowing water guarded the secret of their passage; nor did the pursuers dream at first that Diarmuid, lifting his dear lady high in his strong arms, had borne her in safety across the perilous shallows. But when Fionn found his tracking-men of the Clan Navin at fault he threatened them with death because of the interruption to his journey, so that in fear they waded over the ford, and came upon the brown steeds of Diarmuid and the Princess cropping the short, sweet grass on the farther bank.

'It is even as I deemed,' said Fionn exultingly, 'that they have sought shelter within the Wood of the Two Tents. Now of a certainty shall I discover and destroy them.'

When Oscar and Oisin and Caoilte heard him speak thus they were filled with trouble that his unreasoning hate should move him to this deed; so Oscar called to him by stealth Bran, the hound of Fionn, who loved Diarmuid well-nigh better than his own master, telling him to follow the trail to the Wood of the Two Tents, and bear a warning to the lovers hidden therein.

Now in this wood Diarmuid had built a hut of woven branches for Grainne, and they were resting there when the dog came upon them and thrust his head into Diarmuid's bosom, awakening him. The knight knew that Bran had brought a message of danger, and he said to Grainne—

'Fionn is upon us for the purpose of encompassing my death. It will one day come to me from his hands, for his anger is relentless; therefore I shall not fly, but will bide here to do combat with him.'

An agony of fear fell upon Grainne, and, with tears, she begged him to leave the wood; then, seeing the determination of Diarmuid, she forebode to urge him further. And as they waited a great shout, three times repeated, echoed clearly over the land, startling the birds in their flight and chasing the bloom from the cheek of the listening girl.

Her blue eyes, wide with questioning, sought the brown ones of Diarmuid.

'That is the shout of Fergor, the errand-man of Caoilte, love,' he said, 'and it is my friends who have caused him to utter it, so that I may hear and be forewarned. Yet I will not fly from the approach of Fionn.'

So he set himself to build around his dwelling a fence that no man could pierce, and in it he erected seven narrow doors of strong poles interwoven with saplings to face seven different parts of the wood. And when the Clan Navin had reached the thicket in advance of the others they climbed a high tree, so that they could see the interior of O'Duibhne's fortification, with the fair princess within, a description of whose marvelous beauty they brought back to their master.

'That is in truth she,' said Fionn, 'and glad I am that they are now surrounded.' But Oisin, his son, exclaimed bitterly, 'Thou art surely blinded by jealousy, my father, to think that Diarmuid would linger in this unprotected place knowing that his life is sought by thee.'

'Thou shall hear him give proof of my foreknowledge in his own voice,' Fionn made answer, and going nearer to the fence he cried out—

'Art thou within, O Diarmuid? If so, speak loudly that all may hear thy words.'

And Diarmuid spoke clearly: 'Thou were never in error yet, O chief. We are indeed here, but my arm is still strong enough to keep thee outside my door.'

Then Fionn ranged his men round the enclosure, giving each company a door to guard, and exhorted them to watch closely so that by none of them should the prey escape. From a mound a little way off he observed the hut and saw Diamuid comfort his wife, kissing her three times.

'Now for that,' shrieked the old man in great wrath, 'thou shalt not find even a loophole of deliverance. Thy head shall be my trophy speedily,' and the burning jealousy that was in his heart lit his face with a purple flame.

But Angus of the Boyne, seeing the plight of his foster-son, came to him and passed into the hut unperceived by Fionn and his men. To the lovers he said—

'Come, O dear ones, under my mantle, and I shall bring you both away from this place unseen.'

Yet Diamuid would not accept the proffered aid for himself. 'I shall not run before the pursuit of Fionn, as thou well knowest,' he replied, 'but for my princess it is different. Take her away to safety, O Angus, and if the Fianna should slay me leave her under the protection of her father, King Cormac Mac Art.'

With many sorrowful kissings Grainne bade him fare-well, and, wrapped in the magic mantle of Angus Oge, she passed invisible over the watching companies away to the Wood of the Two Sallows, where they halted to wait for Diarmuid.

Meanwhile, he, left behind, girded on his armour and prepared for battle. He took his tall weapons in his hands and stood meditating in silence for a space. Then he approached one of the seven narrow doors and called—

'Who stands without there?'

'The Clan Baisgne, with Oisin and Oscar,' came in the sweet, clear voice of his friend the Bard. 'Open to us, O brother, and none shall dare molest thee.'

'I thank thee, faithful friends,' said Diarmuid. 'Yet it is by Fionn's door that I must depart, and not by any other,' and he came to the second door, calling:

'Who keeps guard?'

'Caoilte and the Clan Ronan, thy friends. Put thyself in our hands, O Diarmuid.'

'Nay, nay,' he answered, gratefully; 'I should but bring the anger of Fionn upon thee,' and he called to the sentinels of the third door:

'Art thou friends or foes beyond?'

'Thy friends—Conan of the Gray Rushes and the Clan Morna. We love thee, Diarmuid, come to us.'

'Direful would be the rage of Fionn upon thee, Conan, should I avail myself of thy help,' and he spoke at the fourth door:

'What warrior stands here?'

'Thy dear comrade, Cuan, with the Munster Fiana. Thou art of our kindred, Diarmuid, and we will fight to the death for thy sake.'

'Not to thee, O Cuan, shall I go forth to bring thee harm,' and at the fifth door he repeated his question.

'It is the men of Ulster, under the son of Glor of the Loud Voice, who await they coming, O flower of chivalry! Our ranks shall gird thee round, nor shall a hair of thy head by harmed!'

'O noble son of thy father,' said Diarmuid, 'not for worlds would I earn for thee the enmity of Fionn.' Then he went to the sixth door, and the men of the Clan Navin answered him:

'We hate thee, and here we stand to greet thee with our spears—Aedh the Lesser, and Aedh the Tall, and Gonna the Wounder, with all our men.'

But Diarmuid heeded little their bitter speech, save to say, 'No fear of thee have I, O shoeless vagabonds, yet I do

21

not desire to stain my bright steel with the meanness of thy blood.'

At the last door a mighty voice saluted him—

'Greeting from Fionn, the son of Cumhaill, to thee, O Diarmuid. The Leinster Fianna are here to cleave thee to the marrow.'

'This is the door by which I shall pass out, O Fionn,' cried the knight, and rising on his two spears he bounded like a bird over the fence, alighting on the clear space beyond, unseen by any.

Then southward he turned to the Wood of the Two Sallows, where Grainne and Angus bided his coming. To him said the latter when bidding farewell: 'My son, I leave this counsel to guide you when I am gone. Go not into a tree having only one trunk; nor enter a cave with but one opening; never land on an island that has only one channel of approach; where you cook your food do not stay to eat it; where you eat do not sleep; and where you sleep tonight sleep not there tomorrow night.' And Diarmuid promised his foster-father that he would keep this warning in his memory during the days of his life.

*   *   *   *   *

From the Rough Stream of the Champions, where Diarmuid killed a salmon with his spear, they journeyed West, until they reached the Grey Moor of Finnlia. There they met a gigantic man of noble features, to whom Diarmuid spoke, asking his name. The stranger answered graciously that he was called Modan, and was seeking a master whom he might serve by day and watch by night. Thereupon Diarmuid entered into an agreement with him for this purpose, and the three continued their flight to the River of Carra, which flows into Loch Lein. Over this river Modan bore Diarmuid and Grainne with the greatest ease, and beyond it, in a cave hidden in the hillside above the sea of Tonn Toma, they made their resting place. It was their stalwart servitor who caught and broiled for them their food of the

22

salmon, and after he had served them kept watch while they slept.

In the gold and green of the morning Diarmuid went forth to view the territory lest the pursuers should come upon him unawares. As he gazed towards the west he saw a fleet of black ships sailing shorewards, from which a company of nine nines landed. The knight gave greeting at the foot of the hill to them, inquiring from them their race and country.

'From the Iccian Sea, lying between Albion and Gaul, we come,' said the three leaders of the host, 'and we are the three sea-champions, namely, Ducoss, Fincoss, and Trencoss. We have come thither to assist Fionn Mac Cumhaill against Diarmuid O'Duibhne, who has rebelled, and is now a wanderer over the land of Eirinn. We have brought with us three venomous hounds to loose on the track of Diarmuid; fire cannot burn them; weapons cannot wound them; nor can water drown. Now, since we have told thee our mission, perchance thou canst give us tidings of the quarry we seek.'

'I saw him, indeed, but yesterday,' answered the hero, 'and I counsel ye to be wary in the quest, for this Diarmuid O'Duibhne is no common man.' Then he drank wine with them which they had brought from their ships, and after drinking he offered to show them a champion feat.

'It was Diarmuid himself that taught me,' he assured them, 'and I challenge any man of ye to do it after me.'

He brought an empty wine-cask to the crest of the hill, on the edge of a steep cliff, and leaping up on it, he turned it cunningly aside from the cliff to the smooth slope, down which it rolled to the bottom, while he remained standing on it. Three times did he do this for the wonder of the strangers.

But they mocked him, saying, 'Even we shall try your boasted champion feat, until we show our skill and prove its simplicity.' So, one by one, fifty of them tried it in succession, but, not knowing Diarmuid's feint of turning the cask aside from the rock cliff, they went over headlong, and were dashed to pieces on the shore below.

And the next morning, on the same hill, our warrior found the three sea-champions, with their men. To him they again put the same question concerning Diarmuid O'Duibhne, whereupon he said:

'I have seen a man who has met him this very dawn, and now I shall show you another feat he taught me, that you may tremble at a conflict with him.'

He rid himself of his helmet, tunic, and armour, until the shirt was the only covering over his brawny shoulders, and taking the Ga-boi, the spear of Mannanan Mac Lir, he fixed it firmly in the earth, the point standing upwards. Then from a distance he ran towards the spear, rose like a bird into the air, alighted gently on its very point, and leaped to the ground again without hurt or harm of any kind.

Then one of the strangers said, 'Even that feat we shall try to thy downfall, O boaster'; so in succession fifty of them strove to follow Diarmuid; but each man bounded on the point of the spear, which pierced him to the heart. After this great havoc amongst their ranks they bade Diarmuid draw his spear out of the ground, because no other of them should lose his life in trying.

When day had again burst through the heart of the dying night Diarmuid returned to the hill, carrying two strong forked poles cut from the wood. And meeting the three sea-champions yet another time, he offered to show them a great feat of Diarmuid O'Duibhne's. He fixed the poles standing firmly in the earth, and placed the Morallta—that is the long sword of Angus Oge, in the forks, edge upwards, with the point on one and the hilt on the other, binding it securely in its place. Then he rose into the air gracefully like a swift-winged bird, alighted gently on the edge, walked over the sharp weapon three times, and leaped to the ground again without hurt or harm. And he challenged the strangers to try the feat after him.

From their ranks one man stepped forth bravely, saying— 'No champion feat was ever yet done by a man of Eirinn, but that one of us will do the same,' and he bounded up, but came down heavily on the sharp sword, which cut his body into two halves. And in succession the sea-warriors followed his example until full another fifty of them fell by the keen, shining magic blade of Angus.

When in dismay and anger they were about to return to their ships they asked Diarmuid to give them information of the man they sought, that is himself, and he promised to bring them tidings shortly. So in the morning he arose early, and this time arrayed himself for battle in his heavy armour, which was so fashioned that neither through, nor above, nor beneath it, could the wearer be wounded. On his left hip he hung the Morallta, which never left anything for a second blow, and into his hands he took the two famous spears, the Ga-derg and the Ga-boi, from the piercing of which no one ever recovered.

On the shore, at the base of the hill, he again met the strange company, who asked him had he brought them the news they hungered for.

'Diarmuid is not far off,' said the knight, 'I have spoken with him but lately.'

'Lead us to him, O warrior,' cried they all, 'that we may bring his head to Fionn, the son of Cumhaill.'

'I am knit in bonds of friendship to the man ye seek,' replied the other, 'and since he is under the protection of my valour I shall do him no treachery.'

Then in blazing wrath they rushed upon Diarmuid, saying—'Thou art the foe of Fionn, being the friend of Diarmuid O'Duibhne, and we will bring *thy* head also to the Chieftain of the Fianna.'

But Diarmuid's battle-shout rang to the height of the tall hill and along the winding shore, and far away to where the white foamy waves rose and fell in the deep sea, as he drew the Morallta from its sheath and dashed upon them. Asunder he clove them, darting through and under and over them like a wolf among sheep, dealing heavy, vigorous blows with the death-sword until the shore ran red with blood and the watching carrion-birds wheeled lower and lower above their prey. And but a few of all that warlike host escaped from his vengeance to the safety of their ships.

After this he returned to comfort Grainne, who had remained in the cave with Modän, their servitor, wearying for a sight of her lover and husband. Her heart was weak within her at thought of his conflict single-handed against the ferocious champions, but when she saw him ascend towards the cave unhurt and joyous, she ran forward full of gladness to give him greeting. Then Diarmuid told his sweet princess how his good sword and spears had befriended him, while she bent and kissed the blue-black steel for very gratitude.

Yet the battle between Diarmuid and his enemies had not ended, for Ducoss and Fincoss and Trencoss were still alive in the ship on the bay, gazing with dire hate in their souls at the hill that guarded their foe. And when they heard in the early hours of the dawn the challenge of his hollow-sounding shield thundering across the billows, Ducoss straightaway armed himself for combat.

When they met these two great fighters, throwing aside their weapons, rushed upon each other for the wrestle. They twisted and tugged and strained in deadly silence, their sinew crackled, and the veins on their bodies stood out like purple cords; the earth trembled beneath them; they seemed like unto raging lions, or deadly writhing serpents, or like savage bulls that struggle to heave each other with horns interlocked. Thus did they contend until Diarmuid, lifting Ducoss on his shoulder, threw him heavily upon the ground, where he lay groaning; and our hero chained him with hard iron bonds.

Next came Fincoss against Diarmuid, and after him Trencoss, but both of them he overcame easily, and bound them likewise, leaving this speech to them for their solace—

'Your heads should be my trophies, but these bonds are crueller for ye than instant death, and your torment shall be more enduring, since none can release ye from them save myself.'

Then in the security of his cave he gave Grainne tidings of the fray. 'I have left them fettered on the hill so that their pain shall be prolonged, nor is there any fear that they shall be freed from my binding, for only four men in Eirinn can loosen the bonds I tie, namely, Oisin, and Oscar, and Mac Luga, and Conan Maol; nor will one of these four free them. When Fionn hears of their state he will follow us more closely with the three venomous dogs, so we must leave this place to escape him without delay.'

And again they set forth upon their journeying till they reached the broad heathery slopes of Slieve Lougher, where they halted to rest on the banks of a mountain stream that danced and rippled along from the heart of the hillside. From this spot Diarmuid looked down into the valley, and saw approaching it from the westward the foreigners of the sea-champions in battle array, with silken banners waving overhead their ranks. In front of all marched three green-clad warriors, who held the three fierce hounds by three chains, at sight of whose horrid bristling ugliness Diarmuid was filled with loathing. Then Modan lifted Grainne once more, and walked a mile with Diarmuid up the stream into the solitude of the mountain.

Now the reason for the sudden coming of these three green warriors upon Diarmuid's track was because of the advice given them by Derdri of the Black Mountain, an enchantress, and the errand-woman of Fionn, who, travelling speedily over the land to bring the Chieftain tidings of his hunted enemy, had found the three sea-champions lying bound on the hillside above the wave of Tonn Toma. To their lamenting army she spoke, telling them to take the three fierce dogs and follow O'Duibhne, who could not be far off. Which advice they at once complied with.

When the green-clad warriors caught sight of Diarmuid they loosed one of the three hounds on him. The hoarse yelping of this hound awakened great dread in the breast of Grainne, but Modan told her not to fear, for that he would deal with it. Turning round he drew from beneath his girdle a little hound-whelp, which he placed in the palm of his hand. There it stood until the great hound came up raging, with wide-open jaws, when, with a swift spring, the small hound leaped from Modan's hand into the yawning throat of the other, breaking its heart, so that it fell dead upon the spot. And after that the whelp leaped back again on Modan's hand, and the brave servitor placed it under his girdle again.

They walked another mile up the stream, Modan carrying Grainne, whose spirit was in terror lest evil should befall them from the pursuers. Then they heard another time the fierce, hoarse baying of the second hound, and Diarmuid turning said—

'I will try the Ga-derg, the magic spear of Angus, on this hound', and putting his finger into the silken loop of the spear he threw it at the hound, driving its point down the open throat, so that the brute was pierced from mouth to tail and fell dead like its comrade.

Then they climbed another mile into the fastnesses of the mountain, and after them sped the third hound, at sight of which Grainne cried:

'Guard thyself, O love, for this is the fiercest of the three; his eyes are as torching flames, and his teeth are sharp as a battle-brand,' and even as she uttered these words the hound overtook them at a place called Duban's Pillar Stone. Diarmuid stepped in front of his wife to shield her, but the beast rose with one great spring over Diarmuid's head and had almost seized the princess, when the knight grasped him by the two rough hind legs, and, whirling him round, dashed out his brains against a rock.

In an instant he had faced upon the green-clad knights who followed close upon the passage of the hound, and placing his finger into the silken string of the Ga-derg he threw the spear at the foremost of the three and slew him. Then he made another cast with the Ga-boi and brought down the second warrior, and, drawing the Morallta, he sprang nimbly on the third and struck off his head.

Seeing their leaders slain, the foreigners ran hither and thither seeking escape; but Diarmuid fell upon them with sword and spear, dealing death heavily amongst them, scattering and slaughtering. And the news of this terrific conflict was conveyed to Fionn by Derdri of the Black

Mountain, who had been watching near by to the Hill of Allen. He journeyed forth by the shortest ways to the spot where the three champions lay bound, and when he saw the fetters that had been placed upon them by Diarmuid his grief was sore, of a truth, knowing well that no man save the four who lay under *geasa* to Diarmuid that they would not undo his bonds, could untie these strong and flesh-wounding iron knots.

Yet Fionn asked the four in turn to deliver the three sea-kings—Oisin and Oscar, Mac Luga and Conan. They refused, saying, 'None shall be released by us that Diarmuid O'Duibhne hath bound. Fain, indeed, would we place heavier bonds upon his enemies.'

And drawing nearer the great chief, Derdri continued her story of Diarmuid's prowess, relating how he had slain the three fierce hounds and made a slaughter of the foreigners. Hearing which the three kings, being tormented sorely with their fetters, and anguished by the direful import of her tidings, fell back upon the sward and died.

And Fionn caused them to be placed in three wide graves, with Ogham stones laid above them. He gave them funeral rites such as are given to dead kings, and then, filled with an enduring hate and jealousy towards Diarmuid, he marched northward with his host to his home on the broad green slopes of the Hill of Allen.

Then Diarmuid and my Princess, still intent only upon finding a resting-place secure from the vengeance of Fionn, came in their journeying to the Forest of Dooras, in the territory of Hy-Fiachra, and here the knight determined to make an abode for his dear lady, safe in the heart of the leafy shade, quiet and remote.

'Shall we venture into this thick, dark wood, dear love?' said Grainne when they had reached its verge, tired out with the travel of many days. 'I am very weary, and would rest; yet what if Fionn should lurk beyond there and his tracking men?'

'Nay, sweet one,' laughed Diarmuid, 'drive that fear away from thy heart. Fionn would not dare to follow us to the tree of Sharvan the Surly.'

'Tell me of him,' she besought. 'Is he another danger thou hast yet to face?'

'A danger truly if I meddle with the quicken-tree he guards for the de Danaans—his fairy kinsfolk. Otherwise we may dwell in peace anear him. The tree grew up in Dooras from a berry of their sacred food brought from fairyland and dropped unheeded when the de Danaans passed through on their way to Loch Lein for a game of hurley with the Fianna. And hence it came that, hearing afterwards of the growth of this magic tree, the fairy people sent Sharvan the Surly to guard it, so that none might eat the berries save such as were of their own race. For those little red-clusters thou may'st see glowing like a robin's breast among the green leaves, O Grainne, possess the power to change an old man of a hundred years, frail and toothless, into one of thirty, straight and agile and beautiful in form and feature, if he should but eat three of their number. And to the tongue their flavour is sweet as of honey; one who hath tasted them shall feel his spirit grow cheerful as if his lips had dipped into the luscious richness of old mead, and pain and conflict had no longer power to trouble him. Therefore, thou see'st, my fair one, that many would dare danger for sake of plucking three berries of this wonderful tree, but Sharvan sleeps not night nor day; fire cannot burn him nor water drown, nor can any weapon known of man make the least little wound in his body save his own great club, which is tied to an iron girdle round his waist. Three blows of it in a strong hand will leave him silent for evermore—yet what man in Eirinn would willingly seek battle with such as he?'

'Go not near him, O Diarmuid,' said Grainne tearfully, 'save in peace. Thou hast had knowledge of war and unequal combat; now let us have a little quiet home to ourselves under these shadowy boughs.' And Diarmuid consenting, kissed the bright, clear drops from her lovely eyes ere he went to hold parley with the giant-guardian of Dooras.

30

When Sharvan saw the warrior come stepping boldly down the green pathways of the forest he rose up from his seat at the foot of the quicken tree, showing his enormous proportions and the direful ugliness of his dusky face. He was of the wicked race of Cain; his features were thick and sullen, and in the middle of his black forehead gleamed one broad, red, fiery eye. To him Diarmuid spoke bravely, seeking leave to dwell in the forest and hunt its wild animals for food. Whereupon the giant, in brief and surly speech, told him he might hunt or dwell where he would so long as he sought not to lay hands upon the sacred quicken berries.

Without delay Diarmuid built for himself and Grainne a hunting-booth near a spring in the heart of the Forest of Dooras, and round about it, in a clear space, he raised a fence of strong stakes interwoven with tough withes, through which the only passage was one well-barred door. Here they abode in love and peacefulness, drinking the water of the well and eating the food that each day Diarmuid brought down in the chase.

But Fionn Mac Cumhaill had not forgotten his cause of anger against Diarmuid, and night after night he brooded during his sleepless hours over the injury that had been done him by my Princess and her husband. Many were the plans he wove in the dark silence as to how the death of Diarmuid should be encompassed, yet when morning dawned, with its flame of trailing glory in the east, the memory of O'Duibhne's world-famed prowess came back to him, and he knew that by no ordinary means could this man's downfall be assured.

In this wise he kept his hatred active as the fire of fever, and the passion of his bitter mood was at its height when one day there arrived at the palace on the Hill of Allen a strange company of fifty horsemen led by two warriors taller and nobler and more radiantly clad than the others. They bowed low in greeting to Fionn, relating to him in courteous tones the reason of their coming.

'We are thine enemies of the Clan Mac Morna, chieftain, Angus, the son of Art, and Aed, the son of Andala Mac

Morna. Thou did'st outlaw us because our fathers fought against and slew thy father, Cumhaill, at the battle of Knocka, though they afterwards atoned for that crime with their lives at thine own hands. It is not meet that we should suffer longer for sake of this ancient feud, seeing that we are blameless, for we had not opened our eyes upon the earth at the time this harm did happen thee. Therefore, we beg thee now to make peace with us and grant us our fathers' places in the ranks of the Fianna.'

'Even that shall I promise ye,' said Fionn tardily, 'provided ye pay *eric* to me for the death of my father.'

'What may that *eric* be?' they questioned humbly, 'for we have neither gold nor rich garments nor cattle to offer.'

'It is only one of two things, O sons of Morna—namely, the full of my hand of quicken-tree berries or else the head of a warrior whom I hate.'

Then ere they could reply, Oisin the Bard raised his silver voice for their hearkening, and said, 'Take this counsel from me, O sons of Morna, for well I know the thoughts that darken the soul of Fionn, and would warn ye against your own undoing. The head my father seeks is that of Diarmuid O'Duibhne, than whom no braver warrior abides in the land of Eirinn, and little chance would ye have of overthrowing him in combat. As for the berries, O youths, they are those of the quicken-tree of Dooras, which is guarded by a giant, whom even the Fianna hold in dread, and the de Danaan people shall cast their spells upon whosoever seeks to touch its leaves or fruit against their wishes.'

But the two chieftains, in answer to the counselling of Oisin, replied that they had rather pay the *eric* demanded by Fionn than return to their own country again; so they set forth on their quest for the Wood of Dooras and the hunting-booth of Diarmuid and Grainne. When the knight, hearing the sound of their approach had gone forward to meet them, and had learned the object of their mission, he laughed out loud, a clear, deep laughter, at the foolhardiness of the errand they had undertaken.

'I fear ye will find it no easy matter to deprive me of my

head, O sons of Morna, and as for the quicken-berries, Sharvan the Surly keeps a watchful eye upon them night and day. Hath Fionn told ye the tale of this giant—how he cannot be burned with fire, or drowned with water, or wounded with weapons? And which will ye fight for first— my head or the quicken-berries?'

'It is with thee we shall deal first,' said they eagerly.

Then Diarmuid proposed that they should throw aside all their weapons and in this combat rely upon their bodily strength alone. But the wrestle was, indeed, a short one, for he overcame them easily and bound them in close and bitter bonds even as he had bound the three great sea-kings on the hillside above Tonn Toma.

Now this contest between Diarmuid and the Mac Mornas was witnessed by Grainne, upon whom there suddenly came a strong desire to taste the berries of the quicken-tree, and after striving against the craving, at last she told Diarmuid she would surely die unless he brought to her a cluster of the ripe red fruit. The request troubled Diarmuid exceedingly, for he had no wish to quarrel with Sharvan, yet he could not deny his love, seeing the longing that was in her face.

Thereupon the sons of Morna, speaking from the ground, where they lay, exclaimed, 'Loosen our bonds, O hero, and we will go with thee to fight the giant.' And Diarmuid loosed them gladly, for their aid was welcome to him.

At the foot of the fairy-tree they found Sharvan asleep, and Diarmuid dealt him a heavy blow to waken him. He lifted his huge head, glared at the three with his great red eye, saying:

'Art thou come in enmity against me, with whom thou has been at peace, O foolish warrior?' and Diarmuid made answer in this wise:

'It is not in strife I come altogether, but my wife Princess Grainne, the daughter of King Cormac Mac Art, longs to taste of those quicken-berries, and if she does not eat them she will die. Therefore, I pray thee, give me a few that her desire may be satisfied.'

'Nay,' replied the other, 'if she were dying in very truth and one of my berries would avert her death it should not be plucked for her.'

At this a rush of fury filled the heart of Diarmuid, and seeing that he was intent upon fight, the giant struck three great blows at him with his club, which the knight had trouble to ward off and which hurt him sorely. But watching narrowly his chance, he swiftly threw down his sword and spear and sprang upon his foe, taking him unguarded. He clasped his strong arms round the ungainly body, and, heaving him with his shoulder, hurled him with a mighty shock to the earth; then, seizing the ponderous club, he dealt him three powerful blows, dashing out his brains upon the forest leaves.

Weary and aching in every limb, Diarmuid sat down to rest, bidding the sons of Morna drag the slain giant into a secret place of the wood and bury him there, lest Grainne should see and be afraid. Then when at their calling she had come from her house of saplings Diarmuid pointed to the tree:

'The way is clear to the quicken-berries, my dear one. Take thou and eat.' But she replied softly:

'It is only from thy dear hands I shall eat them, beloved.' So Diarmuid, standing up, drew down a glowing branch and filled the little white hands extended towards him. He gave also to the Mac Morna, speaking thus in his generosity.

'Take these berries to Fionn, O youths, and pay your *eric*, telling him, if ye choose, that Sharvan the Surly fell by your prowess alone.'

And they thanked Diarmuid, bidding him farewell, and went their ways to the Hill of Allen, taking with them the one handful stipulated for by Fionn.

Afterwards Diarmuid took Grainne to live in Sharvan's hut among the broad waving branches high above the ground, and they discovered that the topmost berries were the sweetest of all—so sweet and so life-giving that they pined not for other food, but dwelt in peace and bliss in their airy home wrapped in the security of their passionate devotion for one another.

34

When the sons of Morna reached the Palace of Fionn and he asked them had they brought him their *eric*, they handed him the cluster of quicken-berries in answer.

'How came ye to do this deed?' he questioned, looking closely the while at them out of the corners of his keen, shaggy-browed eyes.

'The surly giant of Dooras is slain, O Fionn, and we have brought thee the *eric* demanded for the death of Cumhaill, thy father. Surely that is all it beseemeth thee to know.'

But Fionn smelled the berries three times, and exclaimed:

'It was Diarmuid O'Duibhne who plucked these from the quicken-tree and not ye, untruthful youths, for I know his touch. And well I know it was he, and he alone, who slew the giant. Therefore, it shall avail ye nothing to have brought me these, since ye have made peace with mine enemy, and I shall still hold ye to an *eric* before ye attain to a place in the ranks of the Fianna. But for myself I shall go to the Wood of Dooras to learn if Diarmuid abides in its solitudes.'

So the chieftain took with him the choice men of the seven battalions of the Fianna and marched away to the territory of Hy-Fiachra. They found Diarmuid's tracks to the fairy-tree and eat, until they were satisfied, of the ruddy fruit. Then Fionn, being weary, said:

'We shall rest here until the heat is gone and evening comes, for well I know that Diarmuid O'Duibhne is on high among the branches.'

Said Oisin, 'Truly this jealousy hath tainted thy mind with unworthy suspicions since thou dreamest that Diarmuid would wait for thy approach on this tree knowing that his head is thy quarry.' And Fionn, smiling bitterly, made no reply, but called for a chess-board and men to be brought to him. He and Oisin played the game together until there remained but one move left to the Bard, over which he sat puzzled and silent.

From his seat on a swaying bough Diarmuid had watched the father and son prove their skilful knowledge of chess, but now he felt grieved that Oisin should be the loser, and flinging a berry down with true aim he struck a chessman that Oisin might move it. Thereupon his friend moved the man discreetly and won the game against Fionn.

Immediately they started a new game, which went on until the same pass was reached and the same difficulty had befallen Oisin. And again Diarmuid threw down a berry and struck the right man, and again Oisin moved him and won the game.

A third time the game went on and the chessman was struck by Diarmuid as before, so that Oisin won yet again. Then Fionn gave vent to bitter taunting of his son:

'It is no marvel that thou should'st have beaten me in this game, Oisin, seeing that thou hast acted by the prompting of Diarmuid O'Duibhne.'

'Foolish, indeed, thou art, O Fionn,' spoke Oscar the Valiant, 'to dream that Diarmuid remains within thy reach above on the tree-trunk.'

'Now, say which of us tells truth, Oscar or I, O Diarmuid?' cried Fionn, gazing up into the dark-green shadows.

'Thou, Fionn,' came Diarmuid's familiar voice, like the echo of a clear-toned bell. 'I am here with the Princess Grainne, my wife, in the hut of Sharvan the Surly.'

Then the Fianna, darting eager looks overhead, saw them there together; and when Grainne began to tremble for fear of danger, O'Duibhne put his arm round her and comforted her with three warm kisses before them all.

'Those kisses but add another to the score thou shalt yet pay me,' muttered Fionn between his clenched teeth, 'so now defend thy head if thou art able.' And he offered a suit of armour, arms, and a high place among the Fianna to any man who would climb into the tree and bring him Diarmuid alive or dead.

Garva of Slieve Cua cried out eagerly, 'Let mine be the task, for it was Diarmuid's father, Donn, who slew my father, and I would avenge the deed.'

But Angus Oge learning that his foster-son was in deadly peril travelled to him on the pure cold wind, and without the knowledge of the Fianna came to his aid. His approach brought great joy to the hearts of Grainne and Diarmuid, for Garva was creeping nearer them from branch to branch, and below the eight other Garvas waited to assist their kinsman if he needed help.

When he had well-nigh reached the hut Diarmuid struck him a blow with his foot which dashed him to the ground among the Fianna. And they cut off his head in a trice, because Angus had caused him to take the shape of O'Duibhne, but after he was slain he became like unto himself again, so that all knew it was Garva of Slieve Cua that had been killed.

Then in anger at the death of their chieftain, in succession the eight Garvas tried to destroy Diarmuid, until one by one they met with the same fate—namely, Garva of Slieve Crot, of Slieve Gora, of Slieve Mucka, of Slieve More, of Slieve Luga, of Ath-free, of Slieve Mish, of Drom-more. And the soul of Fionn was harrassed with agony beholding this appalling slaughter.

'Now I shall descend to do combat with mine enemies, O Angus,' said Diarmuid, 'and if I live till evening I shall follow to Brugh of the Boyne, whither thou shalt take my dear one,' and he bade a sorrowful and most loving farewell to Grainne. Angus threw around her his magic mantle, under cover of which they flew away invisible to the watchful Fianna.

The clear voice of Diarmuid was heard speaking then to Fionn:

'Since thou art resolved to encompass my death, why should I fear to meet it now or at any other time? Yet before thou shalt lay me low on the sward, O chieftain, many of thy hirelings shall wend before me through the dark gates. Often in the press of battle did I shelter thee, and when leaving the field I was ever behind, thy shield and thy friend, nor is it meet today that thou should'st be arrayed against me. Yet be it so, I shall not fall tamely nor in dishonour.'

'Truly doth Diarmuid speak,' said Oscar. 'Let him have mercy and forgiveness, for he hath suffered much.'

'Neither peace nor forgiveness shall I grant him,' answered Fionn; 'his head must be *eric* for the injury he hath done me.'

'Shame on thee for that speech,' did Oscar reply to the grim and jealous old man. 'And now I take the body and life of Diarmuid into my keeping, under the protection of my knighthood and valour, so that from henceforth no man in Eirinn dare harm him. Come down in safety, O Diarmuid, my friend and brother; Oscar is here to give pledge for thy keeping.'

Then Diarmuid, walking carefully along a thick branch unseen until he was beyond the circle of the waiting warriors, sprang forward and downward with a graceful airy bound, and alighted outside the host that stood with joined hands round the tree-trunk, and in a moment he was distant from the reach of sword and spear. After him came Oscar, before whose threatening backward glances the pursuing Fianna fell back afraid.

So the two heroes travelled together to Brugh of the Boyne, where Angus and Grainne waited their coming, and Diarmuid's sweet lady almost swooned with joy in her gladness at beholding him again.

The passionate wrath grew yet more active in the soul of Fionn when he saw Oscar and Diarmuid depart together, and he vowed that the latter should not escape his vengeance any longer. Leaving the Wood of Dooras he marched to Allen and gave orders that his best ship should be made ready and provisioned for a voyage. Now this voyage to Tir Tairnngire on which he set forth was to his old nurse, an old woman well skilled in magic, to whom he related his cause of enmity against O'Duibhne, and his will that means should be found to bring his enemy into safe custody. She promised to abet him in his evil designs, and returned with the company to Brugh of the Boyne, enveloped in a thick mist, so that no man in Eirinn knew of their arrival.

It so chanced that Diarmuid hunted alone in the forest that day without Oscar, which being known to the witch-hag, she caused herself to fly into the air by magic on a water-lily leaf, having by her spells turned it into a broad flat millstone with a hole in the middle. She floated straight on, borne along by the clear, cold wind, until she hovered straight above the hero, and began to aim deadly darts at him through the hole. This was the worst distress Diarmuid ever endured, for the darts having had venomous spells breathed over them, stung him through his shield and armour, so that no part of him was likely to escape from their piercing. Seeing that death was, indeed, his portion unless he slew the wicked enchantress, he seized the Ga-derg, and, leaning backward, flung it with sure aim at the millstone. It flew right through the hole, piercing the heart of the hag, who fell lifeless at his feet. He beheaded her and brought the vile head to Angus Oge, relating to him and Grainne the story of their wonderful encounter and his escape.

Angus meanwhile, seeing that the quarrel between Fionn and Diarmuid could not go on in this way for ever, went to the Chieftain of the Fianna and invited him to make peace. Fionn, knowing well that he had been worsted in every attempt made against Diarmuid's life, consented, for he was weary of the quarrel and of the loss of his brave men. Then Angus approached King Cormac Mac Art with the same intentions, and he also agreed to be at peace with O'Duibhne, being sorrowful at the woe and trouble arising from the enmity between these warriors.

Afterwards the Druid returned to Brugh and told Diar-muid the result of his embassy. The latter stipulated that he should be reinstated in his father's possessions and land—namely, the cantred of O'Duibhne without rent or tribute to the King of Eirinn, also the cantred of Ben-Damis—that is, Ducarn of Leinster. These two to be granted to him by Fionn, and a restriction made that neither MacCumhaill nor any of the Fianna were to hunt over them without leave. And from the King of Eirinn he demanded the cantred of Kesh-Corran as dowry with his daughter Grainne.

Again Angus went to Fionn and afterwards to King Cormac Mac Art with these conditions. And they were granted, so that peace was made between all, and the land became once more restful and law-abiding.

Then Diarmuid and Grainne went to live in Kesh-Corran, far away from Fionn and Cormac, building themselves there a house called Rath-Grainne, in which they abode many years in quiet and joy. And in time there came to them four sturdy sons and one little daughter, plenty and prosperity flowed with them, so that people said there was no man of his time so rich in gold and silver and jewels, in sheep and in herds of cattle, as Diarmuid of the Bright Face.

THE DEATH OF DIARMUID O'DUIBHNE

Now, when many happy years had passed over Diarmuid and his wife in their home of Rath-Grainne, in the cantred of Kesh-Corran, a great loneliness fell upon the Princess for a sight of her own people, and she said to Diarmuid—

'Since the wealth of the world has flown upon us, O beloved, and the splendour of our house hath been sung of far and near, it is not meet that the two greatest men in Eirinn—my father, King Cormac, and Fionn Mac Cumhaill—should never have honoured it with their presence, and extolled its beauty and richness. Mine eyes have never met the eyes of my father since that night on which I went away with thee from Tara, and my heart yearns for him and the sound of the voices of mine own kindred.'

'Alas, dear one,' spake Diarmuid, 'this is a fateful wish of thine; for though thy father and Fionn are not at war with me, yet none the less do they harbour enmity in their souls, and for this reason have I made my dwelling far distant from the paths on which they tread.'

'But surely that enmity hath vanished with all the years that have gone over us. Nay, shake not thy head, love, in reproof, for I would that thou shouldst give them a feast in Rath-Grainne, and so, by our trust in them, we shall win back their love and friendship to ourselves once more.'

The sweetness of her flower-face yet held the old glamour for Diarmuid, so, to give his lady pleasure, he consented sorely against his better judgment, and he bade his servitors prepare for the great feast, that it might be given in due magnificence to the illustrious guests and the vast array that should accompany them. The preparations extended over a year, and when all was ready Diarmuid sent messen-

41

gers praying the King to come with his house-folk, and Fionn with the chief men of his Fenian army. So they came, with their followers, their horses and dogs, and abode for a whole year in Rath-Grainne, chasing the dappled deer through the forest, or luring the silvery fishes from the gray stream in daytime, and listening to sweet harp-songs and bardic chanting while twilight trembled upon the verge of night, and night gave way to the first cold quiver of dawning.

It so befell, one night when the year was at its end, that Diarmuid heard in his sleep the distant yelping of a hound, and started up in wakeful alarm, listening. Grainne also heard it, and paled as she threw her arms around him, asking the meaning of the noise.

'It is strange and unwonted to hear at midnight the baying of a hound,' said her husband. 'I must wend forth to learn the cause thereof.'

But Grainne held him closely to her, so that he could not break away from her embrace.

'It is surely a trap laid for thee by the de Danaans, Diarmuid of which Angus of Brugh knoweth not, so may the gods keep thee safely. Turn thee on thy bed again and sleep, and go not near the evil thing.'

A second time the hollow-echoing voice broke upon the stillness of the dark; again Diarmuid made to seek it; and again did Grainne hold him so securely that he dared not go. Then sweet sleep and forgetfulness came to him gently, until for the third time he was wakened by the same sound. It was day-dawn then, and he arose, saying, 'There is now no danger in my going to find this hound, for it is the full light of day.' And Grainne replied, 'Go then, my hero, but take with thee the Morallta, the sword of Manannan Mac Lir, and the Ga-derg—the spear of Angus, so that no mishap may befall thee.'

'But,' said Diarmuid, wishing to make the matter appear of small moment to her, 'surely the Begallta and the Ga-boi shall be sufficient protection to me. Besides, I shall bring my good wise hound Mac-an-Coill, by a chain, and what should I fear when he is with me, and my weapons are in my hand. '

He went forth into the cold air of the morning, never stopping until he had reached the summit of Ben-Gulban. Here to his surprise he found Fionn, to whom he gave no greeting, but asked what chase was on, and who had started it. The other replied—

'It was not I who started this chase, Diarmuid, but some of our Fianna, who, rising out of Rath-Grainne after midnight, chanced upon the track of a wild boar, which they have followed, both men and dogs, though I fain would have held them back. It is no ordinary prey, but the Boar of Ben-Gulban, and they who go after him are bound on a foolish and dangerous pursuit, and already he hath slain thirty of their number this very morning. He is now coming up the mountain towards us with the Fianna fleeing before him, so do thou and I, Diarmuid, avoid his path, and leave this hillock to him.'

'I shall not leave the hillock through fear of any wild boar,' said O'Duibhne, 'rather should it give me pleasure to deal with him in fight.'

'Yet thou are under *geasa* never to hunt him,' Fionn made answer gravely. 'Dost thou not remember?'

'I do not remember. Wherefore was this bond of *geasa* laid upon me, and when?'

'Then I must tell thee of it,' said Fionn, 'for clearly do I recall the circumstance and the manner of its happening. It was when thou were taken, a young child, to Brugh of the Boyne to be fostered by Angus Oge, and the son of Angus' steward was also fostered with thee to be thy playmate. And as price for having his son admitted into such noble company, the steward agreed to send each day to Brugh food and drink for nine men. Therefore, the house of Angus was always open to thy father, Donn, whenever he might choose to visit it, bringing with him eight others to partake of this food and drink. In his absence it was given to the attendants of Angus.

'It so chanced that on a certain day Bran Beag O'Bucan reminded me how it was forbidden by *geasa* that I should

43

sleep more than nine nights at Allen of the broad hill-slopes, and as it was already the tenth morning, I must set out for some hospitable harbourage in which to pass the dark hours of the next night. Thy father came with me to Brugh of Boyne, and there we saw thee, O Diarmuid, surrounded with the tender love of Angus, and happy in the company of thy playmate, who was much beloved by the people of thy foster-father. This aroused a demon of jealousy in the heart of Donn, that the respect due to thee should be shared by another. Not long after that a quarrel arose between two of my staghounds over some broken meat that was thrown them, and the confusion in the hall drove the women and the lesser people in the place to fly in terror. In his fear, thy playmate fled to thy father, creeping between his knees, when Donn, giving the child a mighty, powerful, strong squeeze, killed him on the spot, and cast him under the feet of the staghounds. Afterwards the steward came, and finding his son dead, gave vent to a long and very pitiful cry. Then he approached me and said—

'"Of all the men in this house tonight, O Fionn, I have indeed come worst out of this uproar, since I find my child, and only son, dead before me. Thou dost owe me *eric* for his death, because thy hounds have slain him."

'I bade him examine the body of his son, saying that if he found trace of a hound's tooth thereon I should pay him whatever eric he might demand. He discovered no such trace, but, since the boy's life had been taken, he laid me under fearful bonds of Druidical *geasa* to find out the guilty one. I asked for a chess-board and water to be brought to me, and, having washed my hands, put my thumb under my tooth of wisdom, so that the truth was revealed to me of the death of the boy and the cruel deed done by thy father. Not wishing to make it known, I myself offered *eric*, but the steward demanded I should tell him the revelation that had come to me, and I did so. Whereupon he said—

'"There is no man here who could easier pay me *eric* for this murder than Donn himself. Hear my demand, O Fionn, and Angus, and noble knights. Let the son of Donn be

44

placed between *my* knees to be dealt with as my son was dealt with, and if the lad gets off safe I shall follow the matter up no further."

'At this Angus waxed very wroth, and thy father would have struck off the steward's head but that I intervened. Then the latter, stepping aside, brought forth a magic wand of sorcery and struck his son with it, changing him in the instant into a great bristling wild boar, having neither ears nor tail. He cried out in fierce accents, "I conjure thee, O Boar, to have the same length of life as Diarmuid O'Duibhne, and it is my will that by thee he shall fall at last." As he finished, the savage animal rushed out of the open doorway, nor did one of us note the path he took. In dire trouble, Angus gave thee commands never to hunt a boar, O Diarmuid, and this one now rushing towards us is that same feriocious Boar of Ben-Gulban, so I beg thee now to leave the hill in time lest he meet us here.'

'Not so,' said Diarmuid, 'not so, Fionn. If thou will but lend me thy hound Bran to help my dog Mac-an-Coill, I shall stay to welcome him.'

'I will not leave my hound with thee,' replied Fionn, 'for Bran hath often before chased the Boar, and but barely escaped with his life. Now I shall depart, for here he comes rushing like a demon in fury.'

On the summit of the hillock Diarmuid stood waiting, and suddenly it struck upon his mind that Fionn had planned this encounter for him, so that he might meet his doom. Then the Boar came panting up. Diarmuid slipped Mac-an-Coill from his leash swiftly, but the dog turned tail, and fled far away at sight of the enemy.

'Ah, woe unto him who doth not heed his wife's counsel,' murmured the knight, 'for Grainne bade me at early morn today take with me the Morallta and the Ga-derg, and now I find myself alone and at the mercy of this savage beast, with weapons that do not suit the conflict.'

He put his white, ruddy-nailed finger into the silken string of the Ga-boi and threw it at the Boar, striking him in the centre of his forehead. But no blood issued forth, nor

45

was any wound made in the toughness of his hide. Then O'Duibhne drew the Begallta from its sheath, hitting the Boar a strong heavy stroke across its back. The sword broke into two pieces, yet not one bristle was cut by the blow. The beast made a spring upon Diarmuid, tripping him and lifting him up into the air, so that he fell, as one might sit a horse, astride it. Thus seated, he was carried in a quick wild rush down the hill and far away until they reached the Falls of Assaroe, across which the Boar gave three nimble leaps; but, finding it could not shake off Diarmuid, it bore him back to the crest of the mountain again. Here it gave one mighty cast, and hurled the warrior from its back, when, springing upon him like a flash of lightning, it gored him sorely with its sharp wicked tusks. Yet ere his strength left him, in his woeful extremity, Diarmuid made one blow with the hilt of his sword, which he still chanced to hold in his hand, at the Boar, dashing its brains out. It fell dead beside him on the sward, and here Fionn and the Fianna, coming up shortly afterwards, found them.

Diarmuid lay in the death-agony as Fionn bent over him with bitter speech, saying—the cruel old man—

'It delights me much to see thee in this stress, O Diarmuid, and I would that all the women of Eirinn were gazing upon thee also. Where is thy beauty that won their hearts, and the light of thy brown eyes that drew the blushes up into their soft cheeks? Gone, all gone, and thou art now pale and deformed, with the blemish of the Boar's tusks upon thy straight supple body.'

And Diarmuid, speaking in pain, answered, 'Alas, O Fionn, these words are from thy lips only, not of a surety from thy heart. It is in thy power to heal me if it be thy pleasure.'

'And how should I heal thee?'

'Easily, in truth, for when thou didst receive the gift of foreknowledge at the Boyne, thou didst also receive another gift, namely—That if thou didst give a drink of water from the closed palms of thy hands to anyone wounded or in

46

sickness, he should immediately be healed.'

'And wherefore should I heal thee, Diarmuid? Surely thou of all men doest not deserve it from me.'

'Nay, Fionn, thou well knowest that I do deserve this boon of life from thee,' said Diarmuid, wearily, 'for when thou didst go with the Fianna to the banquet in the house of the Derca, and Carbri of the Liffey and his host surrounded the palace, intent on slaying thee, throwing firebrands over the roof to burn us within the walls, I bade thee sit at the feast, and sallied forth myself to rout them. Heavy was the slaughter I dealt among thy foes that night, and had I asked thee *then* for a drink thou wouldst have given it to me gladly. Just as much do I deserve it now.'

'Didst thou not allure Grainne away from Tara on my bridal night, when I had set thee as guard over her, having full trust in thy fidelity?'

'Not mine the blame, O son of Cumhaill, for Grainne placed upon me heavy *geasa* which I dared not disobey; nor would I have broken through her bonds for all the gold in the world. And the judgments of Oisin and Oscar were with me that night of omen, so it is false what thou sayest of my betrayal of thee. Nor dost thou forget—thy memory holds all things in its caverns—how Midac, the son of Colga, made a feast for thee in the Fairy Palace of the Quicken Trees, and brought secretly to the Palace of the Island the King of the World and the three Kings of the Island of the Torrent, with an immense host, on purpose to destroy thee and the Fianna. And he caused to be placed under thee some clay from the Island of the Torrent, so that thy feet and hands were fastened with foul spells to the ground, and thou couldst not move them, while the King of the World was preparing a host on the Island to come and cut off thy head —helpless as thou wert. It was then that I hurried to thee, O Fionn, and, learning of thy deadly strait in the Palace of the Quicken Trees, went down to the ford to defend it, and engaged in single combat with the three dragon-like Kings of the Island of the Torrent, venturing my life and bearing their attacks for love of thee. Their blood, dripping from their severed heads, broke the spell that sealed thee so miserably to the ground, and had I asked thee for a drink that night thou wouldst not have denied it to me. That is but one of the many difficulties in which I stood thy friend and protector—thy shield and spear. Now, now, when the shadow of death is upon me, I see clearly what before had been unseen. Thou has made foes, O Fionn, many and powerful, and the end is not yet. Shortly there will come dire distress upon the Fianna, yet not for thee do I grieve, but for Oisin and Oscar, and the rest of my fond, faithful comrades. Thou shalt sorely lack me yet, O chieftain, and Oisin shall be lonely through many long years for loss of me.'

Here the sorrowful, angry voice of Oscar interrupted the dying hero, and his eyes flamed through tears at his grand-sire's relentless frown. 'Though I am more nearly akin to thee than to Diarmuid, O Fionn, I will not suffer thee to refuse him a drink in his extremity, nor should any other man who treated him so leave this place alive from the strong hand of my wrath.'

'I know not where there is a well upon this mountain,' said Fionn.

'Untrue is thy speech,' replied Diarmuid, 'for but nine paces from thee is the best well of pure water in the world.'

Straightaway, Fionn went to the well, and, stooping, raised his two hands filled with water; but he had not reached more than half the distance to Diarmuid when he let the water fall.

'It was of thine own will thou didst let it fall, and not by accident, O Fionn,' cried Diarumud; 'that I testify.'

A second time the chieftain of the Fianna went for the life-giving drink, and a second time, when he had reached the same spot, he let it fall, having thought upon Grainne. At sight thereof Diarmuid hove a piteous sigh of anguish, but Oscar thundered, 'If thou does not bring water speed-ily, I swear before my arms that thou shalt not leave this hillock alive,' and Fionn returned to the well the third time, bringing the draught steadily, but ere he reached the spot Diarmuid lay back with a sigh upon the green grass, and life departed from him. Then a wild wailing and three great shouts arose from the Fianna of Eirinn for Diarmuid O'Duibhne. Oscar gazed fiercely upon Fionn, exclaiming, 'Now indeed, hast thou taken from us the noblest heart in all the land—my friend and brother. And would that thou thyself lay dead here instead of him. My grief, my grief— our mainstay in battle is gone for ever. Oh, had I but known that the Boar of Ben Gulban was his enemy, never should this chase have been started today.'

And Oscar wept bitterly, also Oisin and Dering and Mac Luga, for Diarmuid was faithfully loved by all.

'Let us depart,' said Fionn, in the midst of the clamour, 'lest Angus of the Boyne should come and deal us harm for this;' and he went down the slopes of the hill, leading Diarmuid's dog, Mac-an-Coill, in leash beside him. But Oisin and Oscar and Caoilte and MacLuga returned to throw their four mantles about the dead warrior, with many touching words of farewell.

Grainne, watching from the ramparts, saw their home-coming, and Fionn holding Diarmuid's dog in leash. Then a great fear burst forth in her heart, for she knew that were Diarmuid in life this could not happen, and she fell forward in a swoon; but in a little time she awakened out of it, and begged Fionn to give her back the hound, Mac-an-Coill, because it loved her husband, and was his daily companion.

'Indeed, I shall not,' replied the chieftain, 'for it is little enough that I should get even a dog from the hand of Diarmuid O'Duibhne in compensation for all the evil he hath brought upon me.'

'Give her the dog, O father,' Oisin commanded him, 'or those bitter loud cries of lamentation of hers shall ring in thine ears for ever.'

And, stepping forward, he drew the leash from the hand of Fionn, placing it in that of Grainne.

She bade her people go forth up the mountain and bring down the body of her slain knight and lover, so that due rites might be shown him in his burial. And when the company had gone to do her bidding, they found Angus Oge bending in woeful grief above his dead foster-son, for it was revealed to him that Diarmuid had met with the Boar of Ben Gulban, and that the curse had fallen at last. So he came upon the clear cold wind very swiftly to the mountain summit, and when Grainne's people saw him *caoining* there they held out towards him the rough sides of their shields in token of peace. Then together they all raised three loud piercing cries, which were heard in the wastes of the firmament and from end to end of the five provinces of Eirinn.

'Alas, why did I abandon thee even for once, oh son of my soul,' moaned Angus. 'Ever since thou were brought to me, a little clinging child, have I cared for and guarded thee until this black day. And why did I leave thee to the guileful craft of Fionn, O Diarmuid of the Bright Face? Alas, alas, it has been through my neglect thou has suffered. Pity me, oh, pity me, that left my son undefended and in the snare. Yet, never again shall he be apart from me, for now I bid ye, O mourners, to take him up and place him upon this golden bier, so that I may carry him with me to Brugh of Boyne, where, though I cannot restore him to life, I shall bring back his soul into his body each day, and hear once more the silver music of his voice.'

And Grainne's people dared not disobey Angus, so they watched while he caused their master's body to be taken away swiftly, and far from their sight. Then they returned with the message to Grainne, who, grieving sorely at first, grew content in the end that it should be so, knowing the love that was in the heart of Angus for Diarmuid.

*   *   *   *   *

And happy were it for me if I could tell of Grainne's faithfulness to her dead lord and lover, and how the long years of her widowhood passed in tender, regretful memories of him, his valour, and his devotion, who gave up all for love; but, alas, it was not so, nor shall her name be surrounded with a halo of praise, as Deirdre's will be until the ages

50

shall end in Eirinn. For though she drew her children about her after their dead father had been borne to the Palace of Angus, and exhorted them in her sweet, clear voice, 'O, dear children, thy father hath been slain by Fionn Mac Cumhaill against his covenants of peace with him, and now I pray that ye will avenge him well, and I will myself portion out your inheritance among ye, that is, his arms and his armour and his various sharp weapons, that ye may be led to feats of bravery and valour likewise. Go now and learn carefully all practice of warlike skill until ye have reached your full strength, and then return to combat with your father's enemy and mine,' she was the first in after days to revoke the vengeful tenor of her speech.

Fionn, hearing that the youths were pledged to enmity towards him, grew more bitter still in his hatred of the sons of Diarmuid than he had ever been towards their father, but in his plots against them no aid came to him from the Fianna. Rather did Oisin, the silver-tongued, condemn him in reproving eloquence, refusing to lift his sword in this cause, which grieved Fionn exceedingly, since Oisin was his pride and best beloved. Yet the cunning old warrior, well versed in knowledge of the human heart, and more particularly, through long experience, of the heart of a vain woman, saw that only by help of Grainne herself could he hope for peace, and the further support and allegiance of the Fianna, who were almost to a man wroth beyond measure with him for his cruel misdeeds. So he came to her at Rath Grainne, without the cognisance of his army, and greeted her cunningly, craftily, and with sweet words, to which she replied in bitter, sharp-tongued reproach, saying that the sight of him was hateful to her. But Fionn ceased not striving to placate her anger, and continued his gentle loving discourse until he persuaded her to come back with him to his Palace at Allen, where the Fianna were. Oh, fickleness of one woman that shall cast a slur upon all women to the end of time. When the Fianna saw her coming with Fionn through the gates, a willing captive, they raised a great and most insulting shout of derision, so

51

that Grainne bowed her head in shame at the scorn of those warrior eyes.

One only spoke, and it was Oisin. He said, 'Well, we trow, O Fionn, that thou wilt keep Grainne safe *this time* from henceforth. Nor shall any man in Eirinn desire her from thee.'

THE SHEARING OF THE FAIRY FLEECES

The King had listened day after day to the rambling tales that were brought him by the mountain people and the people of the valley, and while he watched the fear that lurked behind their wide-open eyes his own narrowed in thought as to how this panic that had seized upon his subjects could be assuaged. That there was in truth some serious cause for their misery of mind he could not doubt. He had hearkened with them to the bleating of the phantom sheep echoing clear from the high-peaked summits far above; and gazing from the doorway of his royal *dún* he had seen the snow-white flocks moving hither and thither over the heather where the mountain folk had their homes in the mist-wreathed caves. His Druids had sought knowledge from the stars in their night vigils, and returned with awed faces to tell the futility of their research.

'It is not for us to probe, O King, the designs of the Immortals. The hand of Manannan Mac Lir is visible in the heavens, and these are his fairy flocks that appear before the eyes of men but rarely in the passing of the ages. Whether it be for good or evil that he hath shown them to us now we know not, save that it were unwise to meddle with the manifestations of the Gods.'

'Alas! my people are withering away before mine eyes,' said the King, 'and the sick are groaning on their couches while the white fear clutches at their heart-strings. Can nought be done to appease the anger of the Sea-god, or can ye discover wherefore his wrath is turned against us?'

'We shall go back to our vigils, O Monarch, and in the dawning bring thee whatever tidings may be vouchsafed to us,' they answered humbly, wending forth from the royal presence; weary because of their long night watches, yet eager to fathom the mystery of the dread apparition that had caused such woe to the people of Sorcha.

Then the King bent his thoughtful gaze on the kneeling throng, looking longest at the shaggy mountaineers clad in their barbaric garments of fur and hard-tanned leather. Their hair and beards grew in wild profusion, and on their hunting-spear handles were traces of newly dried blood. They began to talk hurriedly, and in uncouth speech, lifting up hands of supplication.

'What is it that ye have seen, and what do ye dread?' said the King to them in soothing wise, and like the roar of a tumbling torrent came the clamour of their words.

'We have heard round our homes at twilight in the high secret places of the hills, O King, the bleating from a great sheep-fold, and when we followed whither it led, we became enveloped in clouds of mist so that many of our number, slipping from the narrow pathways, were dashed to pieces on the rocks below. The bleating and trampling of feet still came to us out of the mist as if a multitude were behind, and when we stretched our arms into it, it broke apart and floated upwards like huge flakes of snow. Now the sound is heard all over the mountains, so that our people are frozen in the horror of a great fear, and dare not venture forth to kill the wild animals that give them food. Our flocks have fled down into the valley, even as we have done, in terror. The hunger is on us, and the sickness hath caught our women and little ones. And the *demnaeoir* (the demons of the air) are shrieking round us in the winds, and the *geinte glindi* (the wild people of the glens) are treading in our footsteps everywhere, until we know not where to go, and for very horror pray the Gods to give us death.'

'And we,' said the dwellers of the valley, 'also live in the shadow of this great fear, O King, for our eyes are ever turned upward towards the mountains, while our fields are left untilled and our work undone because of this cruel fascination that is on us. The *bean-sidhe's* wail is heard from end to end of the valley, chasing sleep from us in the

54

night hours, and the dogs shrink shuddering with bristling hair, when our women would drive them from the hearth-stones into the open day.'

The King moaned wearily, rocking from side to side on his gilded throne. His heart was warm for even the least of his subjects, and his wise ruling had kept peace in the land for many years. This disaster was none of his bringing, nor did one of those fear-drawn faces look at him with eyes of blame.

'When the next dawn breaks,' he said to them in tender tones, 'I shall climb to the summit of those high hills with ye, my children, and if the Gods be kind mayhap Manaanan Mac Lir will grant speech to me. Moreover, my Druids shall offer gifts in propitiation—gold and silver and precious stones—aye holocausts of cattle from my pastures that this curse may be taken off me and mine.'

And kissing the hem of his royal robe they left the hall of audience, hushed into silence by the sorrow in the voice of the King.

The territory of Sorcha lay within a long high chain of mountains which guarded it on east and north and west, but sloped to the south, where the sea broke on a white sandy beach in the shelter of great protecting cliffs. There the King's royal house stood like a sentinel, and from his watch-tower the vast horizon was visible so that no encroachment of hostile ships could come unseen within reach of the land; nor could one single stranger cross the outer boundary unknown to the captains of the army, so closely and minutely was the territory kept secure from foreign invasion. It was through his exceeding care for his people and their lands, that King Feredach had gained his title of the Generous, and wide-spread renown had haloed his name as with a glory.

Now his soul had grown sick within him at the trouble overshadowing his kingdom. He still sat, after the last suppliant had left the hall, brooding over the inexplicable panic that bade fair to turn his beautiful fertile country into waste of loneliness and want. As he leaned forward, his

55

grey beard sweeping his breast, and his eyes glaring glassily downwards, a stranger, entering the wide doorway, came up the rush-strewn floor and bent in salutation before him.

'Hail, O King Feredach,' he said, 'I would have speech with thee.'

The King lifted his eyes and saw a man clad in wonderful garments of colour like the changing skin of the sea-snake, and round his waist a golden snake was coiled for girdle, while over all a mantle of green, with the shifting shining hues of the sea in moonlight, was thrown, which trailed behind him on the floor. His hair was a bright ruddy golden, and on it lay a crown of wondrous sea-weeds still sparkling with the salt-moisture of the deep. His face was young and fair, and open, with clear quick-flashing eyes; and his height was beyond that of any man in Sorcha. In his hand he held a pair of immense glittering sharp shears.

'Who art thou?' said Feredach, 'and how comest thou to pass my guards below, for no man enters my presence unannounced?'

'Not one of thy guards saw me, O King, for they are hiding their faces from the sun, and their ears were deaf to my footfalls. I have travelled far to take from thy people the panic that hath fallen on them.'

'Thy name?'

'My name is but the name of a wanderer, O King, a rover of the sea; a vendor of marvellous silks and curios from many lands. Wherever such are to be found I follow in pursuit; and having heard how thy kingdom is distressed with signs and tokens of the enmity of the Gods, I, who know no fear, have come to find the fairy flock and shear their fleeces so that thy misery may be ended.'

''Twill be death to thee,' said the King, 'since no man can discover them.'

'Yet shall *I* find their hiding-places,' spoke the sea-stranger, 'and do thou bide here on thy throne until I return.'

At the command in his voice the King sat moveless, nor did the guards ranged down the audience-hall seem to see or hear.

56

And while the King waited, sitting erect as a statue of stone, morn gave place to noon, and noon glided gently towards the arms of sunset. Then when the vast portals of the West were opened for the passing of the Day God, the stranger re-entered the palace-hall in the radiance of the fading splendour. In his arms he held, piled high, white masses of finest silky wool, such as had never been seen before in Sorcha, so soft it was, so great in length, so snowy in colour.

He held the fleeces out before the King. 'The blight hath gone from thy people, O Feredach, nor shall the bleating of the flocks molest them more. Thy valleys shall grow green again, and the wild boar return to thy mountains. For me, I go to the Land of Eirinn—to the looms of the de Danaans in the heart of a lonely hill, that an invisible cloak may be woven out of these fleeces for my foster-son, the young Champion of Uladh, Cuchulainn. It shall protect him in battle from wounds, and in peace from sickness; nor shall aught have power over it save the people of the Sea. It has been shorn from the Sheep of Manannan, that roam invisible over many mountains of the world, and whose appearance before the eyes of men is attended with great disaster—through no ill-will of the God's. Fare thee well, O King, my task is finished.'

'Stay, thou wise stranger,' cried Feredach, grasping at the sea-green cloak, but his hand closed upon the empty air, and instead of a footfall there was but faintly heard a placid murmur as of waves breaking upon a pebbly strand.

*   *   *   *   *

'It was Manannan Mac Lir, himself,' said the Druids, blanched with awe. 'It was the Deity of the Waters, for as we looked from the watch-tower we saw a long white narrow wave creep up the shore even to the door of thy *dún*, O King, and on the crest of it rose and fell a silver sea-chariot, with four white swift-footed horses yoked thereto, into which he stepped bearing the fleeces, and while we strained our eyes the white waves subsided into the ocean with a high-splashing of reddened foam as the Sun went through the Golden Gates.'

'Praise to the Gods,' said Feredach.

'Praise. And to thee, O King,' chanted the Druids.

THE KING OF IRELAND'S DEATH-PLACE

The hearth fires were blazing high in the hall of King Mongan, of Rathmore. The flickering torches cast a fitful glare over the listening faces of many warriors who leaned breathlessly forward to catch even the least word that fell from the lips of Dallan Forgiall, the far-famed poet and satirist, and writer of the wonderful elegy on Saint Columcille. He sat on the left hand of the King; the Queen's chair stood to the right, and against its tall carven back Breothigern rested her golden head. Her beautiful eyes were fixed upon the face of the blind poet in never-ceasing wonder at the marvellous tales he unfolded night after night—from Bealtaine to Samhain—for the pleasure of the King.

'There were three kings reigning together in Eirinn for the space of one year—the three Fothad brothers,' Mongan said, breaking a sudden silence, 'and the bards are doubtful as to the death and burial-place of the most famous of the three, Fothad Airgdech. Dost thou know aught of this, O poet?'

'He was slain at Duffry, in Leinster, O King, and buried near the spot where he fell.'

'Not so,' cried the King, interrupting him. 'Not so. It is false enlightenment thou art giving me. He fought his last fight in our own Uladh, and sleeps on a green hillside therein—a fitting place for the King of Ireland's bones to rest.'

Dallan Forgiall rose in fury from his seat. His brow reddened, and his voice was tipped with venom, so that the tumbling, thunderous words could scarce make way.

'And dost thou deny me my knowledge, O King, me who am versed in all that pertains to the history of the dead and the living in Eirinn. Then will I satirise thee, and thy father, thy mother, and thy grandfather, since it is not becoming nor just that thy word should be taken before mine. And I will satirise the waters of thy country so that no fish shall live or be caught in them, and the trees that no fruit may be borne by them, and the plains that they may remain barren of any produce. This will I do, Mongan of Uladh, because of the insult thou hast shown me.'

Here the sweet voice of the Queen broke in upon the ravings of the old man, and her words were like droppings of honey, or the tender piping of a linnet in a hidden woodland bower. 'Nay, nay,' she said soothingly, 'my King hath no desire to wound thee nor vex thy heart with anger or jealousy, O poet. Satirise him not, I pray thee, and thy bronze gift-pot shall be filled with gold and silver and precious jewels—even should I strip my neck and arms of these glittering bands.'

'And I,' said Mongan, 'promise thee the value of seven bondmaids, so that thou cast none of thy spells upon me and mine.'

Dallan Forgiall's face was set in stony anger, and from his lips came forth no sound.

'Twice seven bondmaids; three times seven,' pleaded the King. 'Or if thou wilt, take half my territory—all of it—only let me be free from thy blighting tongue.'

Still the poet sat as a craven image, unmoved by the alluring bribe.

'All I possess,' reiterated Mongan, 'save my own liberty and that of Breothigern, my Queen.'

Then Dallan Forgiall spoke at last. 'One thing hath saved thee, O King—thy wife. She shall be my hostage until the end of three days, and if within that time thou has discovered the death-place of Fothad Airgdech my hold upon her shall be resigned; if no, then I shall come to claim her at the appointed hour.'

For the sake of his honour Mongan consented, but sorrow settled down over Breothigern, and her eyes grew wet.

'Do not grieve, fair one,' said the King, 'help will surely come.'

On the third day they sat waiting, after having in vain sought testimony as to the point at dispute throughout the territory of Uladh. The poet came to enforce his bond.

'Wait until the sun has gone from the heavens,' said Mongan. 'Even yet all is not lost to me.'

Breothigern and he sat together in her bower, and as the hours crept on her tears fell faster. The King bent his head in listening, of a sudden.

'Be not sorrowful, O wife. I hear the tread of one who is coming to our aid. His feet are splashing now through the waters of the Labrinne.' After a little while he spoke again.

'Weep not, weep not. Even now his feet are in the Maine.'

And in another space. 'Take comfort to thee, gentle heart; I hear thy deliverer near at hand. He is crossing Lough Lene—now he is over the Morning-Star River between Ui Fidgente and the Arada; he has passed the Suir on Moy-Fevin, in Munster; his mighty stride hath traversed the Nore, the Barrow, the Liffey, the Boyne, the Dee, the Tuarthesc, Carlingford Lough, the Nid, the Newry River, and behold! he is scattering right and left from him the waves of the Larne Water in front of Rathmore.'

The gray dusk of coming night was gathering round the royal *dún* now, and Dallan Forgiall had renewed his importunities to the King, while the Queen sat, palid and sad in her beauty, by the couch.

'Be not in such haste, thou vengeful bard,' cried Mongan, 'for it is given me to know that thy bond shall be released from thy covetous hand ere long. I see a man approaching the Rath from the South. Even now, by aid of a headless spear-shaft he carries, he hath leapt across the three ramparts as a bird might wing its flight, and now is in the middle of the garth, and now——'

The stranger stood before them. He was taller than the tallest man in the kingdom, and the face of him was young and very fair. His dark cloak was in a fold about him, of strange material and quaintly fashioned, and his hair fell curling to his shoulders.

'What trouble is there on this house?' said he.

61

'A wager I have made, O-stranger, with yonder poet concerning the death-place of Fothad Airgdech, the Ardrigh. He hath said the King sleeps in Duffry, of Leinster—I say it is not so,' answered Mongan.

'It is false history this poet hath been telling,' said the warrior, 'for the monarch lies in a grave not near Leinster nor yet on its borders, but within the borders of Uladh instead.'

'May sorrow overtake thee,' cried the angry poet, 'for that thou has put contradiction upon me. What proof hast thou?'

'Proof in plenty,' replied the warrior, 'which I shall now unfold for the comfort of the King. I was of the army of Fionn Mac Cumhaill, and we were on our return from Alba when we met Fothad Airgdech in battle in the Valley of Ollarva. When the fight was at its fiercest I saw the King standing at the base of a sloping hill watching how the conflict went. Behind a stone, some little distance off, I knelt, and taking careful aim, hurled my spear at him. It passed through him and entered the ground at the other side, leaving its bronze blade firmly in the soil. This,' and he held forth the handle, 'is the handle which was in that spear. The bald rock from which I threw that cast will be found there, and the blade of the spear is still embedded under the grass. The cairn of Fothard Airgdech will be found near it a little towards the east. There is a stone coffin holding what remains of his manhood—on it are his two *Fails* (bracelets) of silver, his *Buinne do At* (twisted hoops), and his *Muintorc* (neck-torque) of silver, and a rock stands as a memorial to him, with an Ogham inscription on the end which is in the ground. What is written on it is this—"Fothad Airgdech is here, who was killed in battle by Caoilte, on the side of Fionn." Our warriors buried him as I have described, and it was by us that his funeral obsequies were performed.'

'Caoilte, didst thou say?' cried the King. 'Art thou, then, that great warrior of the Fianna and kinsman of Fionn Mac Cumhaill himself? By what marvel hast thou returned from the dark halls to clear our doubts away?'

'Because the Fianna ever loved the truth, O King, and beyond the grave we watch the hills and vales of Eirinn as through a mist; growing glad in its joys and sorrowing in its griefs; so when doubt arises as to the past, our hearts ache until it is granted one of us to resume a mortal body and return with wise words of counsel and knowledge to those whom we have left behind. Seek ye the cairn of Fothad Airgdech—all shall be found as I have said—the mouth of Caoilte Mac Ronan knoweth naught of falsehood.'

* * * * *

Mongan found the grave on the green slope,* in the Valley of Ollarva, and near by he recognised the stone from which Caoilte had thrown his cast. On the stone coffin he also found the ornaments of the King—as the warrior of the Fianna had foretold.

He returned to Moylinny—that is Rathmore—with tidings to the Queen, and from henceforth there was no place at his royal board for Dallan Forgiall, nor ever again did Breothigern despoil her white neck and radiant head of gold and jewels at the poet's pleasure.

---

* Now known as Ballyboley Hill, in the Valley of the Sixmile water, where the cairn is to be seen to this day, as well as the stone—a field off—from which the cast was thrown. The country people guard the 'King of Ireland's grave' with due reverence, being careful not to uproot a boulder nor disturb the sloe tree which rises sturdy and wide-spreading over all.

HOW OISIN CONVINCED

PATRICK THE CLERIC

Day after day Oisin kept grumbling at the fare set forth upon the monastery table until the holy men well-nigh lost the patience that was a habit with them. Patrick alone had wisdom to deal gently with the old Pagan whom he had baptised and housed, for with the clearer insight of his pity he saw the woe of loneliness that racked the heart of Fionn's son, and the dread of a future life in which the Christian's God might turn his converted soul aside from the happy land through which the Fianna hunted and revelled beyond the grave. Therefore Patrick spoke softly to him as Oisin held out a shaky massive hand, and pointed scornfully at the large meskin of butter and bannock of bread and quarter of beef that were his daily rations.

'And is it this little portion you offer me, O Cleric; me that am son of Fionn Mac Cumhaill and Bard and Warrior of the Fianna? Why, in my father's house he would have given a larger share to the beggar at his door.'

'I have given more than we can spare, old man,' said Patrick. 'Eat and be thankful that it is not less.'

'My grief,' said Oisin, 'that the days of my father are over, for then an ivy leaf was larger than your bannock of bread, O Patrick, and a rowan berry than your meskin of butter, and a quarter of a blackbird than your quarter of beef. A man could eat his fill nor fear that more should not be forthcoming.'

'Now it is not truth you would be saying, Oisin, my soul,' exclaimed Patrick, 'to tell me these things. Never have I heard of such ivy leaves, or such rowan berries, or such

64

great monstrous blackbirds, even in the wonder times of the Fianna.'

'Yet it was so, and I know where they can be found to this day. Let me go, O Patrick, with my dog, Bran's pup, and a boy to guide me since my sight is dim, and I shall return to your cell with all three of these marvels you deny.'

'Then go,' said Patrick, 'go, Oisin; and oh! grumbling old man, it is empty-handed you will be coming back to me.'

Patrick gave him the boy-guide and brought to him his dog, of which Bran, the hound of Fionn, had been the mother. Now these dogs possessed a sagacity truly marvellous and an affectionateness that almost rivalled human feeling. The Fianna believed that Bran had not always been a four-footed animal, but in earlier times was a man, handsome, supple, and strong, the son of Fair Fergus, the King of Ulster. He had fallen under enchantment, and became the swift, keen-sighted hound, body-guard and faithful companion of Fionn.

So it was accompanied by the pup of this noble hound and a little boy, that Oisin, half-blind and slow of step, with the weight of ages bowing him down, set forth upon his journey. They wandered southwards until they reached the hill called *Cnocan-an-Ein-fionn*, and climbed its slope to the place where is the cave. It was barred by an enormous boulder.

'Roll away the stone that is there, little boy,' said Oisin, 'so that I may enter.'

The boy laughed. 'Ten men could not do it, old man, for it is a great heavy stone and firm in the ground.'

'Lead me close to it.' The boy took the groping hand of Oisin and led him to the stone. Then the old warrior made and easy thrust at it, and the huge block rolled aside, leaving the entrance to the cave open.

'Go into the cave, little boy, and tell me what you see there,' Oisin commanded.

The boy passed through timorously, holding his breath for fear of the shadows. He gazed round in awe.

'I see a great silver horn hanging on the wall, old man,' he cried.

'Bring it to me, little boy.'

'Three men could not lift it, old man, and it will not even move at my touch.'

'Come out and lead me to it.'

Then Oisin took the huge horn down from the wall and held it lovingly. It was the Dord Fianna—the hunting horn of the Fianna.

'Alas,' he moaned, 'many a time have I sounded the hunting-call on thee, O horn of many memories. Oft did my father Fionn waken the echoes with thy music from Loch Lein of the beauty places to Tory of the Kings. My grief that Oisin should live to sound thee and not one of the Fianna left in Eirinn to hear.'

Standing on the hill-top, from whence the sound travelled far and wide, he blew upon it a strong clear note.

From the west a flock of birds came sweeping like a cloud. The boy cried out—

'It is a great flock of blackbirds that are flying towards us, old man. They will be on the hill-top ere long.'

Do you see a fine bird among them, little boy?'

'No, old man, not to say a *fine* bird.'

Oisin raised the Dord Fianna to his lips and blew a second time.

A larger crowd of birds came winging in response.

'Is there a fine bird among these, little boy?' Oisin demanded.

'No,' said the boy, 'not to say a *fine* bird.'

A third time the music of the Dord Fianna pealed from the hill crest over the woods and beyond the shining rivers that threaded the glens and meadows far below.

'What do you see now, little boy?' The boy shrieked in terror. 'I see a huge bird larger than a cow making for us. Let us hide, old man, he is coming swiftly.'

'Loose the pup,' said Oisin.

The lad did so with trembling hands, and the dog leaped forward at the monstrous bird. For hours they fought there

66

on the summit, clawing, biting, rending each other. At last the bird lay dead with claws upturned to the sky.

'Lead me to the bird, little boy,' said Oisin.

But suddenly the dog gave a deep howl of rage, and, mad from the fearful fight he had undergone, rushed towards Oisin with his mouth wide open. From his head a thick cloud of steam arose, and his eyes were like moving balls of red fire in their sockets.

'The pup us coming towards us, old man,' shouted the boy in a panic of fear. 'The madness is on him and the foam falling from his lips. Oh, let us hide. Run, old man, run.'

'Nay, little boy,' said Oisin, 'I will not run. But the dog will kill us unless we kill him first. Take this ball of lead and hurl it into his mouth.'

'O, I cannot,' cried the boy. 'I am afraid.'

'Then place me in his path, little boy.'

So, placed in the dog's path, Oisin met his rush, and hurling the leaden ball with accurate aim it flew into his open mouth and throat. The dog gave a gasp and fell dead.

Then going up to the huge blackbird, Oisin and the boy disjointed him, taking a quarter of him as a proof to Patrick the Cleric. They found the rowan berry and the ivy leaf in the woods of Ballyvalley down by the Shannon River.

Patrick looked long at the three proofs of Oisin's bringing.

'Now I shall ever believe, Oisin my soul, in the truth of the Fianna, though their God was not my God nor their ways my ways. Come, old weary man, to the table. Henceforth your share shall be three times greater than before.'

'Three-quarters of beef, three bannocks of bread, and three meskins of butter?' quieried Oisin.

'Even so, old man,' said Patrick.

THE LAST BATTLE OF ILIACH
OF THE CLANNA RURY

The war-trumpet of Queen Maeve has sent forth its challenge from the borders of Uladh, where she lies encamped with her vast army on its march of invasion into the Northern province. She has come to reave the Brown Bull of Coolney from its pasturage and carry it—the pride of the foray—back with her to the valleys of Connacht as a rival to the famous White Bull which her husband, Ailill, numbers amongst his kingly herds. Her challenge had penetrated to the Court of the Red Branch at Emania, where Conor, the King, reigned nobly and well, but alas! it found the son of Nessa and his brave warriors lying in a state of torpidity under the spells of a woman whom they had, once upon a time, wronged. Macha was her name, and sadly did the Ultonians rue the day on which they condemned her to a trial of speed with the swiftest chariot of the King. Her husband's life was the price of the wife's fleet-footedness, and when the woman, having won, sank down, dying in giving birth to her twin children, before Conor, she laid a bitter curse upon him and his knights because of this evil *eric* they had devised for her undoing. And the curse had wrought itself out in the strange debility which had over-taken them year after year since that day at the same fateful time; so that now, when the red spectre of war came knocking upon their gates and shouting the battle-cry of Connacht in their unheeding ears, they reclined upon their skin-covered couches, half asleep, nor made a move towards the spear and shield that dangled overhead against the wall; nor did even one listless hand stretch gropingly for the short sharp sword that held its place in the leather belt above the thigh of each fallen warrior.

Evil, in truth, was the deed that had brought about this spell on the flower of the Red Branch chivalry; and evil was the curse that had left the borders of Uladh unguarded to the encroachment of a hostile clan. Only the youths who were in training in the great military school of Emania—children of those spell-bound chieftains—bright-faced lads with flowing hair and white unwounded limbs, and the very old fighting men whose day of prowess was over long since, were left to meet the onslaught of the fierce fair Queen and her wild tribes from the Western kingdom.

Yet, of those who were untouched in Uladh by the curse of Macha but two came swiftly towards the Ford of Watching at the challenge of the Connacht marauders. One was in the flower of his youth, smooth-skinned and blue-eyed. His golden curls fell down upon his young shoulders and blew backwards on the wind with the speed of his approach. He wore a shirt and tunic of saffron colour closely fastened around his body with a strong supple belt of leather, and over this was his battle-girdle, also of hard-tanned leather, which encircled him from his hips to his arm-pits, so that neither javelins, nor sharp-pointed irons, nor spears, nor darts could pierce through it, but bounded away from it as if from a rock.

In his right hand he held a tall bronze spear, and on his left arm a great curved black-red shield with a scalloped keen-edged rim, so sharp that whenever he used it as a weapon he cut equally with it as with his spear or sword. As he stood up straight in his chariot behind the flying horses, which guided by the unerring hand of Laegh, his charioteer, bore him like a lightning shaft towards the Ford. Queen Maeve leaning forward in her chariot-seat on the opposite brink of the river, turned her proud eyes, full of questioning, on a tall dark youth who stood near.

'Is it but a boy they send to stay my progress,' she exclaimed in scornful wonder. 'Dost thou know his name, Ferdia? Thou hadst knowledge of the Ultonian lads in thy younger days.'

'I know him, O Queen, and thou wilt find him a foeman worthy of thy steel. Setanta, the son of Sualtainn, was his name ere he was my comrade at the Military School of the Lady Scathach over the seas in Alba. But afterwards, because of a wondrous feat, in which he tore the watch-dog of Culann, the Armourer of King Conor, asunder when it strove to prevent his entrance into the Smith's house in the wake of the King, he hath been called Cuchulainn, that is the Hound of Culann. His strength shall yet be felt in this battle as I and others have felt it in the wrestle, and his feats of championship are many and marvellous.'

'Yet he is but a boy,' repeated the Queen softly, 'a boy, and oh! the pity that against him our javelins shall fly, and our blue sharp-pointed spears be set. Can he be won to us, O Ferdia?'

'Nay, nay, my Queen, he is pledged to Conor, who is his mother's brother; and Cuchulainn was never known to forsake his friend, or break his plighted word.'

While all eyes were fixed upon the young hero, the rumbling noise of another chariot, hastily driven, reached their ears across the Ford. Then a great mocking shout of laughter rose from Maeve and her attendant warriors, and in a moment it had spread throughout the army. A second champion had come to guard the borders of Uladh, and it was at his appearance their mirth had broken forth.

He drove forward to the margin of the Ford beside Cuchulainn, and stayed his horses in full view of the invaders. Their laughter rang louder and longer at nearer sight of him.

Iliach, the Son of Cas, of the Clanna Rury, was his name, and in his youth he had been one of the chief fighters of that royal race. But now, alas, he had grown very old, and being exempted by age from active warfare he had settled down into ways of peace. As he sat by the fireside in his *caiséal*, he fought once more, in memory, the battles of his youth and manhood. The sword that he never hoped to wield again rusted in its scabbard, **his** spears swung idly to and fro upon the wall, the two old steeds that had borne him into the core of conflict many a time and oft, were turned out loose for life into the green, wide-spreading meadows round his home, where the river rippled between high banks of sheltering trees, and the battle-car which had withstood the dint of many a shock in his fierce fighting days was lying, almost decaying, hard by in a corner of his bawn.

Yet, when Iliach heard of the hostile descent upon Uladh, the old war-anger wakened in his heart again, until he felt that the strength had come back to his arm and the keen, far-seeing visions of his dimmed and weary eye. He called his clansmen around him from the high hills and deep glens of that Northern tribeland, exhorting them to follow whither he led, that the Clanna Rury might stand, as it had often stood before, for the defence of Uladh in the face of the enemy.

And while the clansmen were gathering and making ready, the old chieftain, impatient for the fray, set out alone. He had caused the venerable speckled steeds to be yoked once more to the shattered chariot, which had neither cushions nor skins to it, for in his earlier days a warrior looked upon these as luxuries unbefitting his manly hardihood. He slung over his shoulder his rough dark shield of iron with its thick rim of silver, and round his waist, by its leathern girdle, he fastened his gray-tilted heavy-striking sword to his left side. In his hand he took his shaky-headed, many-gapped spears, and because that his armament was ancient and scanty, his people filled the chariot around him with stones and rocks and great flags that he might, with these, defend himself to the last.

It was the sight of this shaggy, strangely-eqipped champion beside the young Cuchulainn that awakened the mirth of the Olne-Machta. Great, indeed, was their merriment as he waved his rusty spear threateningly across the water, and Maeve's shrill womanly laughter rang clearest of all.

'A boy and a dotard—Uladh is, in truth, well guarded.' She stood up in her seat and looked round upon her immense army which darkened the plain as far as eye could reach.

'The Bull of Coolney is mine, O Ailill,' she cried to her husband, 'won without blood or loss, only by this pleasant journey from our own territories to those of King Conor. Let us cross the Ford.'

But, straight as a young poplar, on the other side stood Cuchulainn challenging her bravest to single combat, and on a level with him, Iliach raised his battle-shout of defiance.

Then the fight began, and it shall be related hereafter how the Hound of Uladh kept his guaranty while the Red Branch slept. It is with Iliach of the Clanna Rury our tale is concerned, and how he fought and died.

When the heat of the fray made men pant and strain and wrestle agonisingly in the trial of single combat with Cuchulainn, Iliach held his own against the lesser champions that approached him. The strength of youth had, indeed, been renewed in him, and he fought as in the bygone days, when his name was revered throughout Uladh as that of a warrior of renown. Nay, he fought better than ever in that heroic time, for it seemed as if a magic skill pervaded his being, so quick-darting was he to avoid a blow, so strong was his body to withstand the assaults of those ferocious Connacians, and so supple was the hand that held his long shaky spear as it darted hither and thither under and above the shields of his enemies, piercing, hacking and hewing them until the dead lay piled in heaps around. And when the spear, through excess of use, broke off in two, he mounted his chariot again, and, picking up the heavy large stones with which it was filled, hurled them on the heads of Maeve's men, crushing, grinding, and bruising them until those who had fallen were covered as with a cairn.

Many wounds did he receive with lance and javelin as he stood holding the Ford of Watching with Cuchulainn— many and grievous wounds, through which his life-blood swiftly flowed. And when he felt the icy hand of Death clutch at his heart-strings he groped his way, barely alive, to the spot where Doche Mac Magach, of Connacht, stood, one who had been his brother in arms in their boyhood. Now, they were on different sides in this great encounter.

When Doche saw Iliach approach he went to meet him.

'Well hast thou fought this day, old friend,' said he. 'Yet it has been against heavy odds, and many are the gaping wounds upon thee. Wherefore does thou seek me?'

'To beg thee for one last favour, O Doche Mac Magach,' replied Iliach, 'since my day is over and the night of Death is creeping fast in my track. I have fought my last battle, and no longer can I stand against King Conor's foes. In memory of the friendship that was between thee and me, who never lifted hands against one another until this day, I pray thee grant my request.'

'It is granted, O my friend,' said Doche.

'Then since I would not be led a prisoner to the camp of Queen Maeve, but would rather, of a surety, die upon the field, do thou strike off my head with my sword that I may pass through the Dark Gates speedily and reach the heroes waiting beyond. And yet another favour I would ask, O Doche, that thou wilt convey my sword, now broken and edgeless, to thy friend and mine, Leury of Uladh, as a parting token of my affection.'

'I promise,' said the other, mournfully.

'Then farewell, friend of my heart. Strike swift and sure.'

He knelt on the bloody ground before Doche and bent his withered neck for the blow. Swift and sure it came, and the head of Iliach of the Clanna Rury bounded forward till it reached the feet of Cuchulainn, who saw it without ceasing one moment in his terrible slaughter of his enemies.

'For thee, and for thee,' he cried loudly, 'for thee, and for thee, O brave chieftain, who hath been my mainstay, I shall deal havoc on those who have slain thee.' And the clansmen of Connacht fell as grass falls beneath the scythe of the mower around him, because of his pity for the old warrior whose last battle was done.

*   *   *   *   *

In the Northern Glen on the sea-swept eastern coast of Uladh the Clanna Rury raised the *caoine* for their chieftain, and over his body, which had been tenderly conveyed from the Ford of Watching, they raised the monumental mound.

THE RED WHISTLER

In the land of Eirinn there was no palace so wonderful and so beautiful as the Great House of the Thousands of Soldiers which stood within the Rath of the Kings on the gentle green slope of Tara. Cormac Mac Art had rebuilt it, since the last burning, with added magnificence, until it had become as a vast gem with the glitter of silver and bronze and precious polished woods. Red yew carved and emblazoned with gold made the door posts and the interior of the hall; bronze shutters were to every window; vessels of gold and silver stood tall upon the hospitable board, and over the sitting-place of each warrior hung his well-kept shining arms of valour.

Cormac the King was there in his royal seat, and beside him Fionn Mac Cumhaill. Oisin swept his harp-strings into rousing battle-strains, yet the King heard not; his ear was bent for the fall of fairy feet that came southward from Slieve Cullain, and his heart was sad for the coming destruction of his noble house.

Now, the manner of the burning of Tara was this: Once a year, on the eve of Samhain, the Tuatha de Danaan, who had been vanquished and driven from the land over which they once ruled into rath and hollow hillside, where they had become expert in enchantment and subtle magic arts, came forth into the world again with power over their conquerors. Naught could withstand their fairy craft, nor could all the searching of the stars inspire the Druids as to how this superb palace might be saved from the pitiless tongues of flame blown against it by the de Danaan people.

It was Midna, the chief enchanter, who sent his son Ailinn every year against Tara. He came out from Slieve

75

Cullain in Ulster, whistling the music of sleep on his fedan, and none who listened could keep his eye-lids open. Kings, warriors, and serving-men sank at the table or in the council-hall, and in the dawn of day they wakened unhurt amid the ashes of the ruined splendour.

Cormac had sought advice from Fionn Mac Cumhaill as to how this disaster could be averted, and Fionn, putting his Thumb of Knowledge to his mouth said straightaway,

'I shall seek Fiach Mac Conga, who was a brother-in-arms of my father. A magic spear he hath, and wisdom to guide us aright.'

Said Fiach Mac Conga to Fionn, giving him the magic spear, 'When you hear the fairy music and the sweet-stringed tympan and the melodious-sounding fedan, uncover the blade of this spear and apply its sharp edge to your forehead. Sleep will then keep far from you, until Ailinn comes within reach. Follow him, and he will die like mortal man through the piercing of its flying point.'

This was the comfort Fionn brought to Cormac as they waited on the fateful night for the coming of the Red Whistler. Ears were strained in listening, and the keen, swift-glancing eyes of war-worn nobles grew shadowy with anticipation.

Slowly and sweetly, through the starlight, the music came down the bare arches of the wood.

'I hear my mother's voice,' said an old man, speaking before the King could speak.

'And I the last sob of my son who fell in battle,' said another.

'Ah!' cried Cormac, hiding his paling face in his robe, 'It is a woman's singing voice I hear, and I see the shine of a woman's hair: my first love, and my Heart's Delight, who is dead.'

In the eyes of the Queen horror struggled with drowsiness as an old memory rose and taunted her.

Nearer and nearer the silvern haunting strains approached. Heavier the sleep fell upon shrinking eye-lids.

Said Caoilte slumberously:

'It is a child I am, and my head is laid against my father's knee.' He stretched his huge frame upon the yielding rushes.

And Oisin, with groping fingers across his harpstrings—

'I have a vision. . . her eyes speak. . . she calls my name. . I come. . . I come. . . It is the Land of Youth. . . I come.'

His voice trailed off into forgetfulness.

'Hark, hark, it is the Dord Fianna and the hunting·song,' whispered Goll Mac Morna in his beard, and he, too, passed away into dreaming.

So, one by one, the warriors listened and sank helplessly to the ground. To each the fedan-player bore a message, and where one saw sorrow, another saw joy.

Some there were who saw fear only; fear of a moving battle-place and spouting blood. These shuddered as the fairy sleep overtook them.

'Pierce me, O Spear,' cried Fionn, 'that the enchantment may be withstood.'

Plaintive and wondrously sweet, like an echo over moon-lit waves, he heard tender tones calling.

'It is Berach the Freckled, whom I once wooed,' he groaned. 'Her voice was ever sweeter than the linnet in the springtime.'

Around him it played. His grey hair was stirred by it; he felt the ripples of music on his face.

'Deeper, deeper, O Spear. Bring blood between my eye-lids lest I fail.' And he drove the point into his high wrinkled forehead.

The music was below and above him now, floating into his heart, filling his brain, bearing his soul away on wings.

'O Spear, leap out of my hand that is afraid to pierce deep enough. Pierce thou, O Spear!' and he loosed his hold.

It sank between his brows in a swift bound. The red tide came flowing.

Fionn thrust the stream aside with one hand, and saw, nearing the Royal House, the fairy Whistler.

He was clad in scarlet from head to heel. His hair, coal-black, came curling from beneath a scarlet cap, and his berry-tinted, beardless lips were curved around his fedan.

As he played flames came and went with his breath on the air. So near were they at times that the door-posts were licked with fire. Fionn waited.

The Whistler crossed the threshold, and as he moved on the wavering flames touched Goll Mac Morna's *bratta*.

Then Fionn sprang up with a loud cry, which echoed like peals of thunder in that hall of sleep. The red figure before him seemed made of fire as he chased it through the night. Down the leafless wood, over brown sodden bogs in which its passing shadow danced and glimmered, he tracked it. By its magic potency it crossed, unwet, the wide shining river of Boyne, where Angus dwelt.

It bounded like a blood-soaked arrow from end to end of the grey-green valleys, and glowed as a beacon on the high-crested hills. Close did Fionn follow unafraid. He held the spear in his right hand ready for the cast; he shook the beads of sweat from his hair, which strayed backward on the wind, and on his lips was a prayer to the gods of his fathers.

Faster, faster, O son of Cumhaill, and noble chieftain of the Fianna. Faster, oh faster, for the sombre crown of Slieve Cullain lowers through the dark, and the Tuatha de Danaan are ready to bring thee captive to their underworld.

Faster, oh faster. The spear leaps, bounds, pants between thy fingers; its slender length quivers with life; its point is as a star showing thee the way.

Then Fionn put forth his hunting speed. Swifter than a deer he dashed over the rocky ground, wary as a hawk might swoop upon its prey he tracked the Red Whistler to his lair, and when the rock-door slowly opened in the rugged side of Slieve Cullain he lifted high the hand that held the spear and let it go. It hissed and glittered in its passage through the air, and still hissing and glittering it struck the Red Whistler, piercing him to the marrow. He fell, face downwards, half in and half out of the fairy doorway.

Then Fionn drew nigh cautiously, lest the Tuatha de Danaan might weave their spells about him; and he pulled

78

the spear from the body of Ailinn. When he looked at it there was no blood upon the point, only a moisture that shone with changing hues as dew might under the silver glow of a summer moon.

*   *   *   *   *

Thereafter Cormac Mac Art had peace and joy in Tara. The bards sang the praises of Fionn, and from the meshes of her long fair hair Princess Grainne gazed upon him. The wonder in her eyes was very sweet, so sweet that he felt the quickening of his pulses as in the remote passionate days of his youth.

'Let her be mine, O King,' he said, and Cormac replied,
'Even so.'

Thereat Grainne smiled radiantly in consent, not dreaming yet of a young brown face which was to make her destiny and give to Eirinn the tenderest love-tale that was ever told.

FABLES AND LEGENDS OF IRELAND
Maureen Donegan

A fascinating collection of Ireland's favourite tales including 'The Pillow Talk of Ailill and Maeve', 'The Two Faces of Cuchulainn', 'The Voyage of Malduin', 'The Magic Cloak' and 'Oisín in Tír-na-nÓg.'

LEGENDS OF IRISH WITCHES AND FAIRIES
Patrick Kennedy

From Patrick Kennedy's early youth he felt a deep interest in stories and legends which were peculiar to Ireland. All our superstitions and a great part of our legendary lore, have been handed down to us from our ancestors and Kennedy's dearest wish was that their memory should not fade from the minds of the people. He recorded these fascinating tales of the occult as they were told to him by the people around the fireside.

FOLKTALES OF THE IRISH COUNTRYSIDE
Kevin Danaher

A delightful collection of stories of giants, of ghosts, of wondrous deeds, queer happenings, of fairies and the great kings of Ireland who had beautiful daughters and many problems.

IRISH COUNTRY PEOPLE
Kevin Danaher

Irish Country People is simply one fascinating glorious feast of folklore and interesting sidelights of history recorded without a fraction of a false note or a grain of sentimentality. The topics covered in the twenty essays range over a wide field of history, folklore, mythology and archaeology. There are discussions about cures, curses and charms; lords, labourers and wakes; names, games and ghosts; prayers and fairy tales.